TADEK
AND THE
PRINCESS

A Novella of the Mahisti Dynasty

ALEXANDRA ROWLAND

1st edition 2024

Print ISBN: 978-1-957461-07-6

Ebook ISBN: 978-1-957461-08-3

Contents

I

Now

There were only three portraits of Princess Mihrişah in the palace, all hung in the long, echoing hall of the royal gallery. It had been fifteen years since she'd died, but Tadek still made sure to walk past her portraits regularly, even if he did not always have time to linger with them. He had tried, on several occasions, to sketch a copy of his favorite one to keep in his room in the barracks so that at least he could have enough privacy for a proper visit with her, but he was no great artist, and none of his attempts had turned out. . . right.

But then his Highness whisked the household off to Şirya Manor for his little *honeymoon,* and of course Tadek had to explore the entire house—or rather, nose about in it—and nothing could have prepared him to turn a corner and feel his heart wrench a mile out of his chest at the discovery that his Highness had had a fourth portrait of her, one that Tadek hadn't even *known* about.

It was just. . . there. Hanging above the fireplace in the smaller of the manor's two sitting rooms, directly opposite the door. Tadek stood on the threshold for gods knew how long, just looking at her and hurting, his hand limp and bloodless on the doorknob.

He went in. He shut the door behind him. He stood before her, too wary of his own emotions to let himself feel anything at all except a quivering tightness in his lungs.

It was a good likeness. Possibly an even better likeness than his favorite of the three portraits in the royal gallery. That one was. . . beautiful. It captured her prettiness, her grace and gentleness, her kindliness. But this one had that sparkling light in her eye, that almost-laugh on her lips which his Highness had inherited from her and which shone from his face when he was in a particularly good mood. Everyone said Prince Kadou was the spitting image of his father, and since Prince-Consort Arslan's two portraits hung right next to Princess Mihrişah's, Tadek had studied them enough to know that was true enough—at least when Kadou's face was at rest. But his eyes were hers, and his expressions. His smile. His laugh. The fierce protectiveness of his love. His grace and gentleness and kindliness, of course, those were hers as well. And that sparkle in his eyes when he was happy, and the occasionally impish sense of humor that went with it.

Tadek had been seeing that sparkle more often these last few days since they'd made the trek out from the capital to this most remote of Kadou's holdings. He had to roll his eyes in fond exasperation about *why* that sparkle was in his eyes so often now, but he was glad of it. Glad for his Highness's high spirits. And. . . and glad, because that was a glimpse of *her*, and Tadek had cherished every glimpse of her he'd ever gotten.

He lingered in the sitting room, gazing at the portrait, quivering and fragile all through his chest. He had never had *time* in such abundance, back in the royal gallery, nor privacy, nor the liberty to stare and stare and stare without being questioned by people who couldn't understand.

He could not let himself feel, except to acknowledge that, yes, this one was a good portrait.

2

Then

"Cockroach," Tadek's father said to him, and belched a whole bellyful of beer-breath. "Louse. Rat boy."

"Don't waste your breath," scoffed Tadek's stepmother, tearing the day's charity loaf into five unequal chunks. Tadek got the smallest piece, even though the twins, his half-sisters, were younger than he was—barely old enough to chew the bread themselves. "He's a halfwit."

Tadek was not a halfwit. He was seven, and he had long since learned that everyone got along a lot better when he kept his mouth shut and his eyes lowered.

"Even a halfwit ought to be able to buy a pound of lentils at the market without fucking it up," Tadek's father said, sneering at the chunk of bread that Tadek's stepmother laid on his plate. "I'm supposed to be happy with this? This is supposed to fill my stomach?"

They got a charity loaf every day, but the rest of the food came once a week—eggs, a small round of cheese or butter, a little salted meat or a bag of dried beans, sometimes a few fruits or vegetables, and spices on holidays. Tadek's father hated the charity loaf, because it had bits of potato folded up into it and he said they looked like maggots. He said the sultan had it made that way because he looked down on them for being poor and didn't think they deserved good wheat bread or simit.

Tadek knew his father lied about things sometimes, so he'd asked the clerk who oversaw the charity bakery why they gave out maggot bread instead of nice bread, and the clerk had scowled and looked offended and said that it was because it was healthier and more filling, and that he'd better eat it and thank the gods that the sultan cared enough about the welfare of ungrateful urchins to keep him from starving.

Which was how Tadek learned that the clerks were also liars, because he was hungry most of the time, hungry enough that his stomach hurt and sometimes he felt too sad and tired to play in the street with the other ungrateful urchins. If the sultan really cared, he'd give out more food so they actually had enough. Instead, Tadek's father complained all week that he was dying of hunger, and then when they got their weekly allotment of charity food, he'd eat it all up in two or three meals, barely leaving anything for anyone else. Tadek's stepmother told him not to, but he said a person deserved to eat properly. Tadek often wondered if that meant that his father was the only one who counted as a person. Tadek himself certainly didn't. He'd watch his father gorge himself, and he'd watch his stepmother squirrel away bits and pieces of things so she'd have enough to feed herself and the twins, and Tadek would take his portion of the charity loaf and keep his eyes down and his mouth shut.

Tadek's father had a job. He was a rubbish collector, which kept him out most of the night, and then he'd drink his pay in beer or inhale it in incense lounges, and come home reeking.

Tadek's stepmother had a job too. She was a laundress, which kept her out most of the day. She was shrewder with money—Tadek had followed her once to see what she did with her pay. She'd taken it to her mother's house, and her mother had put it in a jar and hid it under a loose stone by the hearth. That at least explained why the twins sometimes had new clothes. Tadek didn't.

Tadek had a job too. He had several, depending on what he felt like doing.

Sometimes he went down to the docks and picked the pockets of gawping foreigners who tumbled off of merchant ships, but that was more trouble than it was worth. For one thing, the money-changers got suspicious of him when he brought in those funny foreign coins to be made into real money, and for another thing, he was terrified that someday he'd get caught by the fringe guard. As a distant third thing, it didn't feel *fair*, somehow, to bully the foreigners.

Sometimes Tadek went to the house of the blind scholar who lived down the street and did whatever little chores there were around the house. He didn't like that job either, because the scholar smelt of piss and sour, unwashed body—the scholar had mentioned once that he was afraid of going to the public baths, because he might slip on the wet tiles and get hurt.

Sometimes Tadek ran messages. He liked that best of all his jobs, except that there weren't always a lot of messages that needed to go anywhere. The most reliable source of messages were the various government buildings, but they preferred to use cadets from the civil service academy, kids a few years older than Tadek himself who could read and had schooling. But sometimes on very good days, there were no cadets available and someone would poke their head out of the door to see if there were any ungrateful urchins to run a letter across town—and there Tadek was with his best grin and a salute even sharper than the cadets', because it was only at home that he had to keep his eyes down and his mouth shut. He liked that job. He got to run, and he was really fast, and the person at the other end *always* paid him a couple coins, enough to buy a sweetbun or a mug of soup.

Tadek especially liked lurking around the royal Mint, because sometimes they paid him *up front* just for taking the letter, even before he'd delivered it. Double the pay was well worth it, and they had so many messages going in and out that there was almost always a shortage of cadets to deliver them.

But besides that, he just. . . *liked* the Mint. It was a pretty building, and it had shiny brass doors at the front, polished so bright that they looked like gold. He also liked it because of all the *interesting* people that went in and out—ministers and clerks in their various insignia of office, palace kahyalar in their sharply tailored cobalt uniforms. . . sometimes even the sultan himself, arriving in a resplendent carriage drawn by beautiful horses like something out of a wonder-tale. The sultan was an old man, and he was very round around the middle like Tadek's father. The day Tadek had noticed that, he'd stayed well back and he'd kept his eyes down and his mouth shut, just in case.

Cockroach, Tadek's father said, that day that Tadek had been sent to the market for lentils, only to discover that his clothes were so old and worn that the coin his stepmother had given him had fallen out of a hole in his pocket and been lost. *Halfwit,* she had said.

That night as he lay on his mat by the fireplace, a lump of potato bread half the size of his fist sat heavy in his stomach like a rock. He wasn't angry. He hadn't been angry in years. He just felt cold and hard, also like a rock. He didn't like being seven. He wanted to be older. He wanted to be grown-up enough to leave and never come back, and eat all the lovely things he smelled coming from shops and street-carts as he ran messages back and forth. He would leave one day. He had been promising himself that for as long as he could remember.

He was *crushingly* hungry the next day, so he went straight to the Mint and sat himself right on the front doorstep at dawn. He put on his working face with his best grin and said a cheerful and firm hello to all the Mint workers as they went in so that they'd know he had first dibs on messages and that they'd better ask him instead of any nearby cadets if they knew what was good for them. He knew most of their names—he liked memorizing names, and when he knew someone's name, they knew his, and then they usually gave him an extra kür with his message deliveries.

He did indeed get a couple messages that day, early ones before the cadets arrived from up on the palace plateau. When he returned from one of the deliveries just after midday, he saw the beautiful wonder-tale carriage and the pretty horses out in the front that meant the sultan was inside. He was too hungry to melt away into the shadows of the alley until it had gone, so he marched up the front steps and posted himself at the door and waited.

It was a long wait—probably everyone was busy talking to the sultan about his fancy carriage. Tadek crossed his arms and eyed the kahyalar around the carriage. There were seven or eight of them, all in cobalt. Cobalt meant important, everyone knew that. Cobalt meant they were *core*-guard. Tadek didn't know what that meant, really, except that it was the most special that a kahya could be. Most of the kahyalar he saw around the city were fringe-guard, in sky blue uniforms, and usually they ignored him, as long as he was careful. These ones kept eyeing him back as much as he eyed them, so he. . . stopped doing that and kept his mouth shut.

All of a sudden, the doors burst open and someone—a man—burst out in a blur of expensive fabric and expensive smells, leaned on the bench at the opposite side of the door, and threw up into the shrubbery.

A whole flurry of kahyalar whirled out on his heels, pulling his hair back and fussing at his clothing and fumbling at their belts for canteens. "Stand down!" one of them shouted to the others by the carriage. "Probably!"

"Probably?" one of the carriage kahyalar demanded. "What *probably*?"

"Probably in the sense that it's *probably* not poison," said a lady's voice from the doorway, and then the lady herself emerged. "We *did* all tell him that street cart sausages are questionable at best."

Tadek laughed before he could remind himself to keep his eyes down and his mouth shut. The lady glanced over at him with a smile and a twinkle in her dark blue eyes, so it was probably alright for him to have laughed at that. Just in case, he covered his mouth and made a polite bow to her, since she was obviously very important.

"He did say that he didn't care if it made him ill because they looked, and I quote, 'so juicy'," said another lady, coming out behind the first. "It's his own fault, really."

"So much his own fault," the first lady agreed. "We did all tell him. Or at least gave him pointed looks and made tactful comments about the fact that there would probably be things to eat at the Mint which would not make him violently ill."

"*You and I* told him," said the second lady, nodding. "The pointed looks were from the rest."

"My two favorite women, *have some mercy*," the man groaned into the shrubbery, which made both the ladies laugh.

The second lady had dark skin and lots and lots of long braids, and she was dressed in cobalt blue with a sword at her hip and some kind of fancy medal on her chest. A kahya of the core-guard, then, and an important one. Her eyes were black and sharp, and even while she was joking with the first lady, they didn't stop flicking around, as if she were watchful for threats.

The first lady had lighter skin but even darker hair, and she had jewels hanging from her ears and bracelets at her wrist, and she was fanning herself with a jeweled fan, and her clothing was the most magnificent Tadek had ever seen—a rich deep-sea blue kaftan even darker than the cobalt of the kahyalar, embroidered with white and silver and little seed-pearls, and gold-embroidered slippers, and a magnificent headdress with a long veil of some kind of snowy fabric so light that it seemed to float in the barest breeze. Such fancy clothing meant she was even more important that Tadek had first thought. And then there was the carriage. . .

Oh.

Princess Mihrişah—it had to be her, didn't it? Who else would be going around dressed like that and riding in the sultan's own carriage? It had to be her—everyone said the Mahisti family had eyes that strange dark blue color. Tadek knew people with blue eyes, but the difference was as stark as that of the fringe-guards' uniforms compared to the core-guards'.

"I would love to show you some mercy, darling, but I think I'll wait until you're done revisiting the questionable sausage, if that's alright," Mihrişah said airily. "Look how many kahyalar you have around you! I can't even get close. So tragic, beloved, how we have to be separated like this by questionable sausages and attentive kahyalar. They're being so merciful to you already—surely you don't need more mercy from poor Eozena who you ignored so rudely. Nor me, though I obviously have bags of it for you."

"Light of my eyes, this woman. Love her more than life," the man said woozily to one of the kahyalar fussing over him, and added, "My wife is also pretty good," which made both ladies laugh.

"Well, if I'm only *pretty good*, then I'll stay out from underfoot while you're busy being ill, beloved," the princess said. "I'll just sit over here on this other bench with this young man who looks like he probably knows about questionable street cart sausages." She turned promptly in a twirl of blue skirts, marched over, and did as she said she would, smiling at Tadek. "Sorry about my husband," she said cheerfully. "He's a country boy. He doesn't know about questionable street cart sausages."

"There's some that are alright," Tadek said, giving her his best working grin, the one he gave to people who might employ him to carry a message, or to gawping foreigners when they thought they'd just rescued him from a terrible misfortune and before they noticed their purses were gone. "I like the cart with the yellow sides and the red stripe around the border and the green awning. It only made me sick two times."

"Goodness, just two! That's an accomplishment." He nodded, suddenly shy, and her smile warmed. "What's your name, then?"

"Tadek," he said quietly, edging towards the bench and sitting just on the smallest corner of it, hoping that no one would tell him he wasn't allowed. The man—her husband—retched into the bushes again.

"That's a nice name. My name's Mihrişah."

He nodded. "You're the princess."

"I am! And that sick country boy over there is my husband Arslan, the Prince-Consort." She rattled through the names of all the kahyalar around her, starting with the second lady, Eozena ("My second-best friend after that gullible country boy over there") and ending with Navib, who was perched on the driver's seat of the carriage with an intent look on his face as if he were ready to whip the horses into a gallop the very instant he was ordered.

So many names! Tadek memorized all of them. "Hello," he said loudly, so they would all be sure to hear him. "My name is Tadek and I'm the best at running messages. I can run faster than anybody." He nodded. Now they knew that. He turned back to the princess.

"How old are you?" she said, still smiling. "You look just a little older than my son."

"I'm seven," Tadek said. "That's very old, actually."

"It's marvelously old," she agreed. "My little Kadou is six."

"I know that. And Princess Zeliha is, um, nine."

"Ten," the princess said. "It was her birthday a couple months ago. That's what all the fireworks were about, if you remember."

"Yes. I like them."

The princess nodded, still looking very warm and pleasant. "So does she."

"It's my birthday too."

The princess's face lit up so bright that Tadek wanted to lower his eyes because it was suddenly so difficult to look at her face. "What, today?"

He shook his head. "The fireworks day."

"Oh! Well, I'm sure Zeliha won't mind sharing her fireworks with you, then. Happy belated birthday."

He felt his face go hot and he squirmed a little. He'd always secretly pretended the fireworks were for him, and suddenly out of nowhere the *crown princess* was saying that was fine for him to do, as if she'd known that he wanted them.

He supposed he didn't mind sharing them with Princess Zeliha. There *had* been quite a lot of them.

"So, newly turned seven! And such a friendly and outgoing young man," the princess said, tilting her head and looking down at him with another warm smile. "Do you always come to sit at the Mint? You carry messages, you said?"

"Not always. Sometimes I do other things for people."

"Like what?"

Well, he couldn't tell her about the pickpocketing. "Uh. There's a man on the street where I live. He can't see. I sometimes do things for him, like sweeping or dishes. Then he gives me some money, and I—" Oh, he wanted to make her laugh again, he wanted to make her laugh like that sick country boy made her laugh. "I don't buy questionable sausages."

She did laugh at that, a great glittering peal of it with her hand over her mouth, and Prince-Consort Arslan groaned into the bushes again and mumbled something about *no mercy from any corner.*

"A marvelous wit, little one," she said when she composed herself. "Tell me, can you read?"

Read? Why? "No."

"No? You don't go to school?" He shook his head. "Why not? You seem like a very smart young man." He shrugged, and she asked very gently, "Does your family need you to work?"

He didn't want to tell her that he had to feed and clothe himself—not such a beautiful fine lady as her. He grinned at her and kicked his feet. "I like to work."

She smiled, but there was something in her eyes that didn't look quite. . . convinced. "How admirable! And what work would you like to do when you grow up?"

"Running," he said confidently. "Because I'm very fast. And I know all the streets in the city and I never get lost. And I'm good at remembering things."

"Those are all good skills. What sorts of things do you remember?"

"Lots and lots. All the things. The neighbor lady, Madam Darifa, she once said I'm good at names, but Dad calls me a smart aleck when I do that."

"Do you remember faces to go with names?" He nodded, and she pointed to the kahya on the driver's seat of the carriage. "What's his name?"

"Navib," he said immediately. "That's easy, though, you just told me that."

Her eyes sparkled. "I suppose it is easy, isn't it. Well, I bet you can't name the rest, then."

"I can. How much?"

"How about a yira?"

He blinked at her. "That's a lot of money."

"There are a lot of kahyalar, aren't there."

A yira was *silver*. He could eat for *days* off a yira. On the other hand. . . "Can you give it to me in kürler?" he asked dubiously. "If it's a yira, people will think I stole it."

"I'm sure we can manage that. Go on, then, let's hear it." She twinkled at him again, and he almost opened his mouth and rattled off the names then and there, but—

He'd once made a bet with one of the bigger street kids about the results of a race, and then the other kid's friends had tripped him so he'd lost, and beaten him up when he couldn't pay up. "What am I betting, though? I don't have a yira if I lose."

"Smart *and* canny," the princess said with a laugh. "How about if you lose, you'll keep me company until my husband is finished being ill?"

That flustered him so much that he had to look at his feet for a moment before he managed to shoot a glance up at her. "I'd do that anyway, though."

"And I'd give you a yira anyway. Games are more fun, though, aren't they! Come on, stop dawdling or I'll start thinking you're chicken."

He *couldn't* let that happen, so he squared his shoulders and looked over at the kahyalar. "The one on the carriage is Navib like I said. The one who came out after you is Eozena. The one mopping his Highness's forehead is Ayşe." He rattled off the rest easily and looked back at the princess with a firm nod.

She clapped enthusiastically. "Oh, you are good with names, aren't you! Well done, and well earned. Kahyalar, does anyone have a yira's worth of kürler? I'll pay you back."

"I'll pay you back, she says, like we don't all know that the Mahisti are good for it," Eozena said with a wry grin, digging in her pockets. "I've got two or three, I think." It took only a minute for a few more of the crowd of kahyalar to scrape together a fistful of copper coins, which Eozena collected from them and poured into the princess's cupped hands. "Want a handkerchief to tie those up in?"

"Will people think I stole it?" Tadek asked, frowning.

"I'll give him one of mine," said the princess, waving Eozena away. She added, bright as a spring day, "Then if anyone says you stole it, you can just counter-accuse them of treason."

"*Your Highness*," said Eozena, firm as stone.

"Yes, Captain?" the princess said sunnily.

"Treason?"

"Ah, you see, it's because by accusing young Tadek of stealing the crown princess's handkerchief, the person would be insulting the proficiency of the core-guard to prevent such a trivial thing, and therefore denigrating the competency of the civil service as a whole. Doesn't need to stand up in court, you know, just needs to sound scary. Treason sounds scary, don't you think?"

Eozena gave the princess a long, slow blink and said, "As you say, your Highness."

The princess had a beautiful little embroidered pouch at her belt, from which she produced a handkerchief to wrap the coins up neatly. "You know, Tadek, if you learned to read, you could try taking the entrance exams for the academy. There are plenty of opportunities for a smart young man who likes to work hard and is so good at remembering names. Isn't that right, darling?" she said as Prince-Consort Arslan straightened up and washed his mouth out with a swig from Ayşe's canteen.

The prince-consort spat into the bushes and wiped his mouth with the back of his hand. "Absolutely correct. I haven't the foggiest notion what we're discussing, though."

"Whether young Tadek here should learn to read and take the exams for the academy."

"I hear it's a marvelous opportunity for a young person's advancement," he said, taking a damp cloth from another kahya—Affenür—and wiping his face and beard. "Not that I would know. Personally, I recommend marrying up." That made the princess laugh again.

"I don't think I want to get married," Tadek said. The princess dropped the little bundle of coins in his hands and he squirreled it away into his kaftan quickly as the prince-consort crossed over and took the princess's hand, raising it to his lips to kiss her knuckles.

"Think about the academy, then," the princess said, tearing her eyes and her smile away from her husband to grace Tadek with them briefly before she got to her feet. "We'll be coming back to visit the Mint again on the first day of the month. I'd love to speak to you again if you're around then."

"Yes, your Highness," Tadek said, nodding energetically.

"Good. It was nice to meet you. Spend your winnings wisely!" She looped her arm through the prince-consort's and they went down the steps. She shot the prince-consort a sly, sideways smile and nudged him with her elbow. Tadek pretended to be occupied with his coins, but he listened very closely as she leaned close to her husband. "Shall we bring our little shy one along next time?"

The prince-consort sighed and murmured, almost too quiet for Tadek to hear, "I've said before, beloved, that it might go better if we find him playmates who are more like him. The outgoing ones get bored too quick, and I think he can tell."

"Young Tadek would be gentle with him."

"You know this after a five minute conversation?"

"Well—" she said, but by then he was handing her up into the carriage and climbing in after her, and the rest was cut off by the closing carriage door.

3

Now

On the rare occasion when there was no one else in the royal gallery, Tadek always bowed to her portrait when he arrived and again when he left. He made it floridly ostentatious, because that had made her laugh, and those moments had been his proudest achievements.

When there *were* other people in the gallery, he restricted himself to a quiet, subtle salute with his fist over his heart and his head lowered, as if he was departing his post at the shift change when it would have been improper to interrupt any important people having their important conversations.

He bowed to her when he left the little sitting room, that first day at Şirya Manor—not ostentatious, but *deep* and sincere, and he held it until the base of his spine ached and his hamstrings burned and his injured leg screamed a bit.

The second day, he brought a flower he'd picked from the fields outside, and he laid it on the mantelpiece under the gilt frame, and he squared up his shoulders and gave her a proper bow, florid and fancy and just a bit rakish. He'd developed all kinds of new tricks since the last time he'd seen her alive, and he thought they would have made her smile.

He rose, tucked his hands behind his back in parade rest, ignored the ache in his leg, and looked at her.

He couldn't make himself speak, at first. Then he felt foolish about it, and fiercely glad that he never let anyone see more than that subtle fist-to-heart salute.

Even before she'd died, back when he'd been an academy cadet, he'd snuck into the gallery to talk to her portrait sometimes. He'd liked talking to her, and he could never do it as often as he wanted to, because. . . because she'd been the crown princess, and he'd been just a child. She had duties; he had studies and work.

He went to the royal gallery to visit her more frequently after she died. He'd gone every time he advanced to the next year of schooling, every time he got an academic award or a commendation. . . He'd gone when he'd been promoted to the fringe-guard and then, finally, to the core-guard. He'd told her when he'd been appointed to the service of her son—he told her after the first time he *kissed* her son, because Tadek damn well knew that Kadou wasn't likely to confess things like that to her, and a mother ought to know.

He'd made her all sorts of promises over the years. He'd fought to keep as many of them as he could, and he knew that she would have forgiven him for the ones he couldn't.

It took a long time, that second day, before he was able to find the right words and speak them.

He began softly: "Doing my best, ma'am."

That had been the first promise, and it was the only one that mattered.

After several moments of silence, he added, "Your son's a bit of an idiot, you know, but he's so pretty nobody notices. Good news is that he's found a matching idiot. They're nauseatingly in love. They're off at the other end of the house, having sex for the fourth time today."

Would she have giggled at that? Would she have spluttered and waved him off and laughingly said that there were some things a mother didn't need to know?

Maybe he should have kept it to the important part. "He's happy," Tadek said softly. "He's really, really happy."

That, at least, she would certainly want to know.

4

Then

"Will you teach me to read?" he asked the blind scholar the day after he'd met the princess. He had his fistful of kürler from her Highness, wrapped in her handkerchief—*hers!* He'd been dazed with astonishment for the rest of the day, and he'd kept hiding in alleys to take it out of his pocket, rubbing the fine fabric between his fingers and tracing the embroidery around the hems to remind himself that it was real, that *she* was real, that she'd *spoken* to him.

It was enough money that he wouldn't need to work for a little while to keep himself fed, though he did worry that going too long without doing any message-running might make people start to forget his face.

Perhaps he just had to make a bet with himself. Her Highness thought he was smart—she! Her Highness, the Crown Princess Mihrişah!—so surely it was worth the risk to *try.*

"Eh?" said Scholar Alichan. "Why don't you just go to school?"

"I'm in a hurry." He only had his fistful of kürler, and once they were gone, he'd have to go back to working for most of the day so that he could eat. (But her Highness was coming back to the Mint in a month—would she make another bet with him, and give him another yira's worth of copper? Would she help, if he asked?)

"Learning can't come in a hurry, lad," the scholar snorted. He settled himself in his chair. It had layers and layers of blankets which had been laid over it and sat upon until the scholar had made a perfect little hollow of a nest in it. It was stained and grubby and very smelly, but he didn't want anyone to wash it because it had taken so long to get just right. "What's got a thorn under your saddle about reading all of a sudden?"

"Nothing, really," said Tadek, shrugging. The scholar might have been able to see that—he could still see some light and shadows, apparently, and Tadek was standing between him and the window while he scraped the broom across the floor. He wasn't sure if he trusted the scholar not to tell anyone if Tadek confided what had happened. He wanted to guard all of that jealously from his father, his stepmother, his half-sisters. He wanted to clutch it close to his heart with her Highness's handkerchief, something that was *his* which couldn't be snatched away and torn into chunks and given to everyone else but him, just like the charity bread.

He wondered if Scholar Alichan had ever taken the merit exams himself, and if he'd tell Tadek what they were like, and whether Tadek had to do anything else besides learn to read to make it there. Her Highness had said he could do it. She'd said it, and she was kind and pretty and she'd laughed at his jokes.

And she'd asked him what he wanted to do when he grew up. He could barely conceive of it. To him, being grown up meant being able to *leave,* to get away, to be a person. He'd get his own ration of charity bread and the rest of the food, and he'd make it last all week—unlike his father—so that he never went hungry.

"Do kahyalar get charity bread?" he asked before he could think better of it.

"What? No. They get paid, lad. Coin. And. . ." The scholar waved his hand. "Rations. Room and board and pay, all of that. And a stipend for learning."

Tadek thought about this. He scraped the rough, worn bristles of the broom across the floor, tumbling crumbs of bread and dustbunnies back and forth in front of him. He wasn't paying much attention to the cleaning. "What does stipend mean?"

"Money, but money that you can only spend on a few things."

"Oh. But money besides that, for pay?"

"Yes."

"Oh."

The scholar squinted in his direction. "Why are you asking about the kahyalar, boy?"

"I just wondered what they eat. My family gets the charity food. And you do. So I just wondered."

"Kahyalar, and reading," the scholar muttered. "Not thinking of the academy, are you?"

"No, not really," Tadek said quickly. "Just wanted to read so I could carry messages better. Then people could write down where I should take it to, and it'd be faster than telling me directions."

The scholar grunted. "Well. I'm not going to give you reading lessons for free. You don't do chores in my house for free, and I don't teach for free. That's fair, isn't it?"

"Could I exchange chores for lessons?"

"No." The scholar sniffed. "I don't need my house cleaned every day, but boys your age are all blockheads and won't learn a thing unless it's hammered into your head with a mallet on a daily basis. So. Five kürler every day you want a lesson."

"*Five?*" He could eat for two whole days on five kürler! Three if he didn't mind being a little hungry.

"You're the one wanting the lessons," the scholar said sharply. "I went to the University of Thorikou, you know. I'm very learned. Five kürler is the cost."

That would eat through his one yira's worth of copper astonishingly fast. He'd just have to learn fast too.

On the first day of his lessons with Scholar Alichan, Tadek sat beside him (trying to breathe shallowly to keep from choking at the stench) and watched intently as the scholar wrote out the alphabet in a shaky hand on an old wax tablet. Tadek never forgot a face, and letters were a lot like faces, as it turned out, and they had names just like people. So: he looked at the faces of the letters and listened to the names Scholar Alichan gave each one and fixed them both in his mind.

The scholar said, "Now, here is the first word for you to learn," and he wrote: Teh, Ah, Deh, Eh, Keh—

"Tadek," said Tadek immediately. "That's my name!"

"Hm," said Scholar Alichan, as if disapproving. "Paying *attention*, were you? Fine. Try this." He wrote again: Heh, Ah, Seh, Ee, Reh, Ah.

It was a bit longer than Tadek's name, but he could remember the names of a whole crowd of kahyalar. He mouthed through the letters one by one. "Hhh. Hah, see—hasee. Rr . . . Ra—Hasira!" His family name.

Scholar Alichan did not seem at all pleased. "Making a fool of me, boy? Coming in here begging for lessons, trying to play a *trick* on me? Get out."

"I wasn't," Tadek said, not really surprised. Grown-ups didn't like it when he did things well—except her Highness. She'd liked it when he'd shown her how good he was at remembering the names of all her kahyalar.

"Get *out!*" the scholar shouted, and Tadek sighed and trudged out the door.

He had the letters' names and faces in his head, at least, and so then all he had to do was practice them until he knew them by heart. He mouthed them to himself as he lay on his straw mat in front of the hearth. The twins slept in a little bed with a faded old curtain around it on one side of the room, and on the other side, Tadek's father and stepmother had a bed only a little bigger with an equally faded curtain.

Tadek preferred the straw mat by the hearth because it was warmer, but it did mean that on cold nights, sometimes someone would sit up and hiss at him to poke up the fire or add another handful of twigs—Tadek's father didn't like them using full logs at night. He said it was too expensive. If Tadek was already asleep, sometimes they'd throw a slipper at him to wake him up. He got the warm hearth spot, so he had the duty to keep it tended at night.

He didn't mind it. He watched the little licks and flickers of flame curl over the sticks. Sometimes they made the shape of a letter, and he silently mouthed its name to himself and tried to think of as many words as he could that had that sound in them.

During the day when he was running messages, he looked for signs with writing on them and tried to read them letter by letter, but sometimes the words had been painted so swishily and ornately that he had trouble recognizing the letters' faces, and he had to jog onwards.

He spent five of his kürler on a book from a secondhand shop—worth a whole lesson, was it? But it was longer than he could have gotten through in one lesson, so it was a better bargain—and spent another ten on a bigger kaftan from the secondhand shop, since his old one was looking *very* shabby and getting short on his wrists again. He wanted to look nice for her Highness when he next saw her. He wanted to show her that he could read, that he could *learn*, and that he could be as neat and tidy as the kahyalar. He wanted to tell her that he was going to take the exams, and study hard, and be a core-guard of the kahyalar so that he could spend all day following her around and protecting her from—from—from questionable street cart sausages. Or protecting her husband from them, anyway, since he was the one who needed it more. She seemed to like him very much, so Tadek decided to like him too.

He kept track of the days carefully, counting them out until the end of the month. Her handkerchief had gotten grubby by then from being in Tadek's pocket all the time, and from being constantly touched, and from a few times when he'd accidentally dropped it in the dust. He washed it as carefully as he could, just in case she wanted it back, but he was too scared of tearing it to launder it the way his stepmother washed clothes by beating them up on a washboard with a paddle.

The morning her Highness had said she'd go to the Mint, Tadek got up very early, before dawn, and went to the bathhouse, where he spent the very last kür he'd been hoarding to wash himself as clean as could be. He'd been planning on just using water and steam since soap cost more, but when a bleary, yawning man left his pot of soap unattended while he took a dip in the steaming pool, Tadek couldn't help but sidle over and filch a finger-scoop of it.

It brought an astonishing amount of grime out of his hair.

He dressed in his new kaftan, which he hadn't worn yet so that it would be nice and clean for seeing her Highness, and he combed his hair with his fingers, and then he went out to the lady of the bathhouse, burst into tears at her, and told her he'd lost the ribbon he used to tie his hair and he'd gone through the whole bathhouse but couldn't find it. She clucked at him in disapproval and told him to be more careful, but she also took a box of things out from under the counter which had the word "LOST" written on the side and picked through it. She grunted and pulled out a somewhat dusty, wrinkled blue ribbon. "This one's been in here for ages. You can keep it."

Tadek sniffled his thanks at her and scampered out with it clutched in his fist. Blue! A blue ribbon! What fortune! He'd only been hoping for a bit of string, but a *blue* ribbon! It wasn't remotely Mahisti blue—a few shades too greeny-teal for that—but it was undeniably *sort of blue* and that's what counted.

He jogged to the Mint, his stomach grumbling with hunger, and arrived just as the carriage was pulling up. His heart leapt into his throat, and he stood there shaking as the crowd of kahyalar all dismounted and helped her Highness out of the carriage. Across the street, a dog tied to a hitching post barked like mad at the horses, but Tadek was so fixated that he could barely hear it. He felt terribly shy, and all he could think was, desperately, whether if she'd even remember him. Perhaps she'd just been nice last time, perhaps she wasn't expecting to see him again. . .

She glanced around as she alighted—and like a miracle, when her eyes caught on him, she *smiled*. "Good morning, Tadek!" she said brightly as she came up the steps. "My, you're looking very handsome and well put-together today! I think you must have grown an inch since the last time I saw you."

He could have fallen over in relief, but he bowed instead, with all the flourishes that he'd once seen a street actor do during one of the festivals. "Thank you, your Highness."

"And such pretty manners! Your mother must be very proud of you." Tadek's face as he straightened must have given something away, because the princess said, "Oh no, what did I say?"

"Nothing. She's dead, that's all."

"Oh. I'm so sorry." After a moment, she added, "Well, I'm sure she's still very proud of you—the Lord of Trials will be telling her all about how well you're doing. They just want you to try your hardest, you know, and I think you do that already."

He hung his head, his eyes stinging, and nodded. "Yes, your Highness."

"There, good boy. I have some appointments inside, but I'll have a few minutes to talk afterwards, if you'd like to. And I was wondering if you could do me a favor."

He looked up sharply. "Yes. Yes, your Highness, anything."

"I wanted to bring my little Kadou along so you could play together while I'm busy, but he has the sniffles today, so he couldn't come. I was thinking it would cheer him up if someone drew him a picture as a get-well present. I brought paper and things, if you'd like to try."

"Alright," Tadek said solemnly. He'd never drawn a picture before, except with rocks in the mud or the burnt end of a stick against the plaster of an alley wall. It couldn't be all that different. The princess smiled brilliantly at him, which made it all worth it, and nodded to one of the kahyalar—Navib—who got a lap-desk sized box out of the carriage. "I'll do my best, I promise."

"I'll see you in a little bit, then!" the princess said. "Thank you!"

Tadek bowed to her again as she swept inside.

The lap desk was the fancy sort with hinges to a storage compartment, which held sheets of paper and some sticks of what seemed like pure color. Tadek poked them—they were hard and a little dusty, and they left strangely bright smears of color on his fingertips. "What are these?"

"Pastels," said Navib. "You can use them like bits of charcoal."

"Oh. Thank you." Her Highness wanted a picture, so Tadek would draw the best picture he could. The dog across the street was still yelping furiously at the horses, and each piercing bark echoed off the cobbles and the stones of the buildings and made it awfully hard to concentrate. But the Lord of Trials—and more importantly, her Highness—only wanted him to do his best.

He drew Her Highness with her blue eyes and her long hair and her sweeping blue robes, and then he drew Prince-Consort Arslan next to her—much less detailed, but then Tadek had mostly seen the backside of him while he'd been throwing up in the bushes—and then a smaller figure between them to be Prince Kadou.

Then he painstakingly wrote out *get well soon* underneath, one letter at a time. They got kind of cramped towards the end, because he'd started writing too big and he ran into the edge of the paper.

He finished and looked up at Navib, who was standing nearby and watching curiously. "I'm done."

"Can I see it?"

Tadek shook his head and held it to his chest—carefully, so the pastels wouldn't smudge, as he'd so swiftly learned that they would if he so much as brushed against them. He didn't want to show it to anyone but her Highness. Navib was her kahya, and he had a friendly face, but. . . A lot of adults had friendly faces at first, and stopped being friendly when Tadek did something they didn't like.

"Alright," said Navib. "You can keep drawing, if you want to. Her Highness won't mind."

Tadek looked down at the lap desk. There was plenty of paper in there, and lots of the pastels, but they were probably expensive. They *looked* expensive. He'd never seen colors so bright or paper so smooth, or a box so nicely made. The hinges didn't even creak when he opened it. He'd already used a lot of the pastels to draw the picture, and he didn't want to use them all up. They didn't belong to him, after all, and it was rude to use something expensive that was someone else's. He would sooner have died than done something to make her Highness angry at him.

"No thank you," he said. Navib shrugged and took the lap desk back to the carriage, leaving Tadek clutching his picture.

Her Highness came back out before the dog had gotten tired of barking. She smiled at Tadek and came right over to sit beside him on the bench. "How long do I have until we have to get going?" she said to a nearby kahya who Tadek hadn't been introduced to last time.

"Fifteen minutes or so, my lady," said the kahya.

"Wonderful, that's plenty of time to catch up!" she said, turning to Tadek. "Did you draw a beautiful picture?"

He looked down at it, holding it so she couldn't see it, and his heart fell into his feet. It wasn't very beautiful. There were a lot of colors on it, and a lot of smudging, and her Highness looked like she had black noodles on her head instead of hair, and Prince-Consort Arslan's hair looked like sticks, and their clothes were just strange blobs… He chewed his lip and looked up at her, pleading. "No. I'm sorry."

"No?" she gasped, surprised. "I'm sure that's not true. Can I see it?"

Of course she could. He would have done anything for her. He lowered the picture to his lap so she could see it, and she leaned a little closer.

"What do you mean *no*, Tadek!" she said immediately. "It's a beautiful picture. Aw, it's me and Arslan and Kadou, isn't it? It's *sweet*. And did you write that yourself?" He nodded miserably. "You couldn't read last time, right? But you learned so quickly that you could write that? Tadek, that's *wonderful*."

He looked at it again. Was it wonderful? He couldn't tell. His eyes welled up with tears; he scrubbed them away with the back of his hand.

Her Highness touched his shoulder. "Tadek, sweetheart, it's lovely. It is. Did you try your hardest?" He nodded, too choked up to speak. "Then that means it's the best picture you've ever made, isn't it? Logically." He pressed his hands to his face and gave the smallest nod. "Then Kadou will be *so happy* to have it, I know it."

"Thank you," he said, his breath hitching and hitching. He didn't want to cry in front of her. He didn't want to. Her kahyalar probably never cried in front of her. Adults didn't like that kind of thing. "If he doesn't want it—"

"If he doesn't want it, then I'll keep it for myself, because *I* like it very much," the princess said firmly. "I think it's beautiful, because you made it and you tried really hard." She rubbed his back a little. "You did your best work, and I'm proud of you."

He didn't know what to say. "Thank you," he said again, and sniffled mightily.

"I'm so surprised you learned to read and write so fast," she said, pulling the picture very gently and slowly out of his lap and onto hers. "You spelled everything right, too! You must have been practicing a lot."

"I bought a book," he said, his breath still hitching now and then. "With—with the money you gave me. I bought a book and—and I try to read it."

"A book! What a sensible and responsible purchase. What kind of a book is it?"

"It's about a man with, um, a chicken statue, I think? And he's taking it to a party."

"A chicken statue?"

"A small one. He has it in his pocket, I think." She still looked puzzled. "It's a chicken and it's made of stone?" He said, uncertain. "Maybe it's just colored like stone—but it said hard like stone, so I don't know."

Her Highness got a very strange look on her face. "Ah. . . What's the title of this book?"

"*The Ravishing City.*" He sniffled. "That was a big word, *ravishing,* but I read it all by myself. I asked Scholar Alichan what it meant and he said it means beautiful."

Her Highness had gone pink, touching her fingertips to her mouth. "I see. And. . . how much of this book have you read, dear?"

Tadek wiped his cheeks on his sleeve. "Only a couple pages."

"Thank the gods," she said fervently. "I think you should maybe set that book aside until you're a little older, sweetheart."

He looked up at her in alarm. "But I need to practice—it cost *ten kürler!*"

"I know, I know," she said, wincing. "I'll give you another yira and you can buy another book, alright? But you have to ask the bookseller to help you pick it out."

Tadek shook his head feverishly. "No, Highness, no, clerks trick you into buying expensive things."

"You bought that book because it was cheap?"

"Yes. And it has woodcut in the front of a man who looks cool." He had a flower and a secret smirk and he was very handsome, and Tadek liked to look at him. He probably would have gotten farther in the book if he hadn't spent so much time looking at the woodcut in the front.

"You can look at the woodcut all you want, but you really ought to be older before you read that type of book," she said firmly. "Save it for later, alright?"

"But why?"

"It's about grownups."

"I'm practically a grownup. Almost."

"You're seven, if I recall correctly. It's about grownups doing grownup things."

He thought about this for a long minute and scowled. "Oh. Then it's about sex? That's *boring*."

"Yes," she said quickly. "Very boring. You wouldn't be interested in reading about that."

"I spent *ten kürler* on it and it's *boring*?" He looked up at her, grumpy and beseeching. "Highness, can't you make that illegal?"

She burst out laughing.

All too soon, one of the kahyalar cleared his throat, interrupting the enthusiastic story Tadek was telling about the time the baker's wife fell face-first into a big pile of dough, and said, "Highness, we'll need to be leaving soon."

"Oh," said the princess, her face falling. "Thank you, Çan. Can you get me one yira's worth of kür, please?" She sighed a little and turned back to Tadek. "I've been meaning to ask whether you thought about doing the exams?"

He nodded. "I want to. I really want to. But I don't know what else to do besides learn to read and write."

"That's all you need," she said, reassuring. "Having more schooling than that is good, but not necessary. The exams are just to see how hard you can work and how smart you are and how much you want to join the academy and why. If you can't do sums or if you don't know *The Ten Pillars of War* by heart, that doesn't mean you won't get in."

Sums and the ten pillars of war, whatever those were. Maybe the bookseller would know about those, or Scholar Alichan. "Alright."

"You can ask any kahya you see on the street when the exams are and they'll tell you," she said. "They happen twice a year. I think the next one is in two months, so you might want to wait and take the next one."

"Eight months?" he said, dismayed.

"Oh, you can do little sums too! Two and six is eight, that's right! See, you'll do marvelously—if you feel like you'll be ready to take the ones in two months, you can. And if you don't get in, you can always try again as many times as you want." She stood, and he hopped to his feet as well. She smiled down at him. "I need to leave now, but it was nice to see you."

"Are you coming back next month?"

She shook her head sadly. "Arslan and I are going out to the country for our anniversary next month. If you're at the next exams, I'll see you then—and if not, I'll leave a message for you here at the Mint for the next time I'll come by, and I'll try to bring little Kadouçiğim so you can play with him."

Çan the kahya came back with another fistful of kürler. As he poured it into her Highness's hands, he cleared his throat and said with a casual shrug, "There might be a bit more than one yira there, I didn't count carefully." She beamed at him, which only made Tadek a little bit jealous, but his heart was breaking too much for him to be all that bothered.

"Do you have the handkerchief still?" she said, crouching before him. He nodded and pulled it out with a sniffle. "You're taking very good care of it, I see," she said warmly as they put the coins in it and tied it up. "There, don't cry, little one. You'll be alright. I expect to hear the rest of the story about the baker's wife next time we visit, alright?"

He nodded sadly, and her Highness stood as the kahyalar brought their horses around and started to mount up. Another stood at the carriage door waiting for her.

That dog across the street had not stopped barking, and evidently it found the mounting of the horses utterly intolerable—there was a cry on the other side of the carriages, and two of the horses reared as the dog was suddenly *amongst* them with the collar around its neck nowhere to be seen, snarling and snapping at the horses, darting in between them, leaping at the kahyalar—

The whole thing lasted only a split second: Çan flung himself at the dog and caught it by the scruff of the neck and one arm around its chest, dragging it back across the street while three or four more kahyalar followed and helped secure it by its collar again.

Tadek found himself in front of her Highness, his heart thundering, his arms held wide, panting for breath and shaking all over. He felt a little sick with fear. That dog hadn't been all that big—barely hip height on Tadek—but it had seemed *monstrous* for a moment, a beast with huge fangs and a slavering ferocity. His mind had flashed *danger,* but instead of scrambling for safety, he'd flung himself in front of her Highness. He hadn't even thought about it. He'd just—*moved.*

He looked over his shoulder at her, his eyes wide, his limbs weak, his eyes stinging with tears again—but his terror ran out of him abruptly at the sight of her eyes *shining* like they were.

"Are you alright, my lady?" Çan said, jogging back around the carriage. He paused at the tableau. "Oh."

"I'm alright," said her Highness, smiling and smiling. "Tadek protected me."

Çan leaned against the carriage and grinned down at Tadek too. "So he did. Well done, young man. You've got your priorities straight."

"That was the sweetest thing I've ever seen," said Ayşe. "Look at him! What a brave little mite! That's a baby core-guard if ever I've seen one."

"Agreed, absolutely," said Çan. "You can't train instincts like that. Ever thought of taking the academy exams, kid?"

Tadek swallowed all his fear and bowed to Çan. "Yes sir. Two months from now."

"Good man. What's your name?"

"Tadek Hasira!"

"Well, hopefully-future-Cadet Hasira, I should think you'll have a couple of good letters of recommendation in your exam files," Çan said with a little wink as he handed her Highness up into the carriage. "Come up to the palace the day before the exams and ask for me, and I'll help make sure you're ready."

"Attaboy," her Highness murmured, which made Çan laugh, and Tadek *couldn't* be jealous about that.

5

Now

He visited her every day, because if the two idiots could take advantage of all the privacy out here in the ass end of nowhere so they could screw like it was about to be banned, then Tadek could do the same in regards to his own small pleasures.

It was a pleasure to be able to spend time with her, even if it hurt his heart and made his eyes sting sometimes.

He should have known that he'd eventually get caught, but by then he was *hoping* for it. There were too many words welling up in his throat and too much of a burden on his shoulders, and it didn't feel fair to spill it all to *her*.

It was the second idiot, thank the gods. If it had been Kadou, then Tadek would have had to cover it up and *pretend*, because that was his *mother* and it wasn't Tadek's place to make him deal with Tadek's own hurt. (His *grief*, he made himself think. That's what it was, wasn't it. Call a spade a spade.) But it was Evemer, thank the gods twice over and thrice. Somewhere during those days of visits, as Tadek stood in the same spot in perfect parade rest no matter how his leg hurt him, looking up at her and memorizing every brushstroke, he'd had the thought that, of all people under the sky, Evemerwould *understand* in a way that nobody else would.

He knew it was Evemer just from the rhythm of his footsteps in the hallway. Tadek didn't move when the latch clicked and the knob turned behind him.

Let him see, if he's going to see, he thought. His feet hurt, and his leg hurt, and his lower back hurt, and he didn't *care*. It was the least she deserved. It was the damn least. Why not let Evemer see? He was Kadou's husband, and so Tadek was his armsman—and Evemer Hoşkadem was Evemer Hoşkadem, the only one who would really, really understand. Why not let him see?

There was a silence, as if Evemer had paused on the threshold, just as Tadek had when he'd first opened the door to this room. Then, the creak of that one worn floorboard just inside, and the soft whine of the hinges, the snick of the latch again. The pad of footsteps across the rug to Tadek's side.

Tadek said nothing. He held parade rest and the gaze of her beautiful painted eyes.

Evemer said nothing, of course. Not a man of many words. But Tadek could almost *feel* the weight of Evemer's eyes on the portrait. . . on the wilted collection of common field daisies that had accumulated on the mantelpiece with today's fresh one cheerfully atop the pile. . . on Tadek's uncharacteristically rigid and formal posture.

"It's a good portrait," Evemer said at long last, when Tadek did not fill the silence himself.

"It's the best of them, I think," Tadek murmured back.

There was another long silence. Evemer was so very good at silences—judgmental silences, astonished silences. . . horny silences, apparently, as Tadek had discovered a couple times on the trip out from the capital when they'd stopped by some pond or brook to rest and water the horses in the sweltering summer heat and Kadou had decided to bathe. Evemer was still, ostensibly, his Highness's kahya, and so he was of course *obligated* to watch. Horny silences were funny. Tadek had teased him unmercifully about it.

This silence was a companionable one, Tadek thought. A respectful one.

Tadek stirred himself. "Was his Highness looking for me?"

"We were curious about where you'd gone off to. He wishes to go for a ride, and he thought you might enjoy coming along." Another silence, this one distinctly tactful. "Shall I tell him you're occupied?"

"No," Tadek said. "No, I'll come."

"It is not urgent. He's eating."

If they hadn't been right in front of *her,* Tadek would have taken the opportunity to tease Evemer about how Kadou *always* got hungry after sex and how surprised Tadek was that they hadn't chafed their dicks off yet.

After a long moment, Tadek asked softly, "Where were you? When you heard."

Where were you when you heard? There was no further need to clarify, not with the context of *her* hanging above them. It had been a refrain amongst the kahyalar for a decade and a half now whenever Princess Mihrişah and Prince-Consort Arslan came up in conversation. The refrain had begun to peter off in recent years, not *always* asked, but the question was familiar enough that it would be a long, long time before it faded from memory.

"At combat lessons with Master Agabos," Evemer said. "We were learning shield drills. Someone ran up to him at the side of the field. We thought it was just one of the usual messages, so we waited there in formation."

"What happened?"

"The messenger spoke to him. Master Agabos screamed and fell to his knees. He wept. We. . . watched. We didn't know if we were allowed to break formation. The others around me were frightened." There was another long pause. "I was too, so I told them not to move. Holding formation was the only thing I knew was right to do. We were all twelve or so."

"He was a good teacher."

"They all were." Silence. "Where were you?"

Tadek took a long, slow breath. "I was studying. I had an exam the next day. I didn't hear for hours."

"I never saw you studying."

"No one did. That was the point." He released his breath. "I used to hide in the dormitory attic with my books." It had been important for nobody to know how hard he had to work. *I'll do my best*, he'd promised her Highness, and so he'd *needed* everyone to think that his best was effortless, that he was always doing it. Then no one but him would know whether he was disappointing her. "I came down for dinner and the sergeants were handing out those oxblood armbands. I walked up to Sergeant Barada and said, 'Wow, who died?'" Out of the corner of his eyes, Tadek saw Evemer wince. "Yeah. I thought she was going to slap me. Then she said, 'Her Highness and the Prince-Consort.'" Slow, measured inhale. "I didn't speak another word for twelve days." Long, controlled exhale. "That's not the story I usually tell people when they ask that question."

"Oh?"

"Usually I say that I heard when I was getting my first kiss."

Evemer gave the smallest, softest snort. "That seems more like you."

"Yes. I know."

Silence, silence, silence.

"You were one of the last to stop wearing the armband," Evemer said. "I remember that."

Tadek smiled, his heart wrenching. "You remember thinking it was unseemly for me to be in mourning that long for someone else's mother."

Silence. "Yes," Evemer said softly.

"Thought so."

"Sorry."

Tadek shrugged one shoulder. "It's not like we knew each other in those days." Evemer had joined up a little late, so Tadek had been ahead of him in classes, inasmuch as these things were measured. People advanced when they advanced, and Tadek had been trying for five years to advance as quickly as possible. Evemer had joined up at ten or eleven, if Tadek recalled correctly, though he'd had come in with more schooling and hadn't had to catch up very much. The gap between them had widened as the years went on—Evemer had probably trusted his teachers to tell him when he was ready for the exams, instead of hurling himself at them the moment that *he* felt like he could pass. "I wasn't ready to take it off, even when I did."

Evemer made some soft hum of acknowledgment.

Silence.

Tadek wasn't going to speak again. He would answer questions, but he would not fill this uncomfortable silence. He wished fiercely for Evemer to *feel* the discomfort, so he'd *know*, so he'd *understand*.

. .

"You admired her," Evemer said.

"We all admired her," Tadek countered.

"You loved her."

"We all loved her."

Silence. "What was she to you, then?"

There, Tadek thought. There it was. The right question. The question no one else had ever asked him.

He made a parade-perfect quarter-pivot to Evemer on the heel of his uninjured leg and looked frankly at him. "You want to know?"

Evemer turned to mirror him, a little more slowly. He'd fallen into parade-rest too, but that wasn't remarkable. He seemed to default to it most of the time, whether he was on duty or not. He studied Tadek for a long moment, and Tadek waited until Evemer said, gentle and formal and *clearly* like he'd been taking lessons from Kadou, "If you'd like to tell me, armsman, then yes, I do want to know."

"Alright," Tadek said. He felt shaky. Quivering through the very core of him, now that he'd come to this moment when someone *finally, finally* asked him the question that he'd been silently answering for two decades of his life. "Listen carefully."

Evemer went very still and fixed his eyes and attention on Tadek as intensely as he ever did for Kadou.

Tadek tilted his head toward the door. "His Highness," he said. He hesitated just a moment, swallowing hard to clear the lump from his throat. Then he tipped his head toward the portrait. "*My lady.*"

Evemer was already still and solemn, but his expression somehow fell immediately into *grave*. He swallowed too, and nodded once, and Tadek pivoted right back to the portrait.

Silence.

Evemer just kept standing there. Tadek could hear his breathing—a little unsteady.

Evemer Hoşkadem, of all people, would understand. Evemer Hoşkadem, Evemer Mahisti-eş, who addressed Kadou as *my lord* like it was the tenderest thing you could call a person, like that was simply the label for the most precious thing that Evemer could possibly conceive of. Evemer, who looked at his lord like he was the north star that Evemer had been following faithfully all his life, and who now had to look at Tadek and realize that *his* star had flickered out long ago and left him lost in the dark. *Remember you are mortal,* as the old adage said. Or, perhaps more specifically: *Remember your lord is mortal, the same as my lady was—just fucking imagine how that feels.*

Evemer's hand fell on Tadek's shoulder, warm and heavy, and then he just *kept* it there. Not like he was trying to pull Tadek away from her. Not like he was trying to push Tadek in a different direction. Just. . . there. Heavy. As heavy as the weight of Kadou's protection had felt when Tadek had heard that his Highness had begged the sultan to lay Tadek's life in his hands. Tadek couldn't bear to shrug Evemer off, and the shaky feeling in his core grew more fragile, and the silence—fuck, he couldn't stand a silence, he couldn't *stand* it, how could he think that he could go to toe-to-toe with Evemer Mahisti-eş in a silence competition—

"Say something," Tadek said sharply.

"I understand," Evemer said quietly. A moment later, he said, speaking (as Tadek knew) from the very foundations of his heart, "I'm sorry for your loss."

Tadek had been waiting fifteen fucking years for someone to say that to him. He shattered.

6

Then

The exams were easy.

Tadek already knew addition and subtraction with great speed, from having to count and recount his money and figure out how many days he could survive on however many coins.

The instructors in charge of overseeing the exams showed him a map of Araşt and asked him to label as many cities, regions, landmarks, and geographical features as he could—Tadek didn't know any of that except that the sea was the Sea of Serpents. But when they showed him a map of Kasaba City, he snatched it away from them and pointed out every district and told them the sort of people who lived there. He could identify all the major roads, a great many of the minor roads, the location of the Mint, the Shipbuilder's Guild and six other guilds, all twenty-three of the big markets and what they were known for, the gates of the city, the palace (obviously)—

At that point, they'd pried the map out of his hands, given him a blank slate and a piece of chalk, and asked him to *draw* the map of the city from memory and explain it all again, which he promptly did. The drawing wasn't quite to scale, but he explained that as he went along: "This street goes through Little Tash, but it should be longer and it's not because it's running into the foreign quarter that I already drew—" They asked him how quick it would take to get from the palace down to the Shipbuilder's Guild and back, and he held forth for a length of time that surprised even him about how it depended on the time of day and the season and whether there was a festival because of how that affected the amount of traffic on the Lifeblood, the main road through the city which everyone thought was always going to be the fastest way to anywhere, and then he explained three other ways of getting there by backroads and alleyways and across a rooftop that would get him there as just fast during the day as it'd take on the Lifeblood at night when there was almost no traffic to speak of at all.

They asked him to read a page of something, which he did with determination even when he hesitated and stumbled over his words and had to stop for a long time to sound things out.

They made him play a game with a bunch of cards laid facedown on the table and explained that he had to turn them over one by one and find matching pairs. He *loved* that game because it was just remembering faces, and he tore through it so fast that the examiner raised her eyebrows and made a note on her paper and said that he'd *gone for the jugular on that one*, whatever that meant.

They asked him about books he'd read. He told them that his favorite book was *The Ten Pillars Of War* and that he'd saved up his money to buy a copy. He offered to recite the pillars by heart, because he'd learned what they were: the leader, the plan of attack, knowledge and intelligence, allies and troops, economics, cunning strategies, weapons and war machines, defensible positions, an understanding of the terrain, and avoiding direct conflict (and, for some reason, a chapter called "Admonishments to the Would-be

Righteous Man", which seemed like it was mostly a jumbled basket of little pieces of advice that weren't significant enough to qualify as a whole *pillar* of wisdom). Tadek did not mention *The Ravishing City*, which he had peeked through as soon as he'd gotten home from the Mint, that second time he'd visited with her Highness—it had some later woodcuts in it which had made him scrunch up his nose and roll his eyes. Kissing looked gross, and sex looked even more gross. He was still annoyed that he'd bought such a boring book.

The examiners made him run around a big loop in the open-air gymnasium and training grounds outside the palace to see how fast he could go, so he ran like he'd been paid a full altın to get a message across town as quick as possible.

They took him to a long pond at one end of the training grounds and told him to swim to the end and back. Tadek didn't know how to swim, but he threw himself in with the handful of other children and figured it out as he went.

They took him to a room full of clean bedsheets that had been hung to dry and told him to fold one neatly.

They took him to a room, empty except for a chair and a table, on which was placed a plate with a single gorgeous, luscious, golden-baked sweetbun dripping with honey. They sat him right in front of it and told him he could eat the sweetbun now, or he could wait until the examiners came back and have *two*, and then they walked out. Tadek found this very strange, but two sweetbuns would keep him full *all day*, and he felt like there was probably some kind of trick involved here, like maybe the sweetbun was poison or he'd get in trouble for stealing, so he kept his hands off it. The examiner did give him two sweetbuns when she came back, though, *and* a tray with a lot of food on it, so maybe there wasn't any trick at all.

Finally, they put him into a room with a lot of other children, and they gave him a piece of paper and a dip pen, and told him to put his name at the top carefully because he was going to write an essay. Tadek had been expecting that, because Çan had showed him how the night before—it was just explaining what he meant and then providing examples to prove he was right. Tadek found a desk to sit at, and the examiners announced to everyone that the theme of the essay was "the meaning of loyalty". Well! That was easy. There was a lot about that kind of thing in *The Ten Pillars of War*, which he'd read in bits and pieces in the bookseller's shop across a period of several weeks because it was too expensive for him to buy a copy of his own. Tadek wrote that loyalty was like a family where everyone made sure that everyone got enough to eat, and no one took more than their fair share, except sometimes you gave up your share if someone else needed it more, and that was okay because other times you'd get a little more when you needed it. Tadek wrote about his own family, which did not have any loyalty in it, which you could tell because of how the charity bread was divided, and he talked about meeting her Highness, and how she'd given him money to buy books so that he could learn to read and become the very best kahya and protect her from terrifying ravenous wolves and street cart vendors of questionable sausages.

It was a whole day of exams, ones that made sense and ones that were very strange, and at the end of it, they were all given *another* meal. Tadek had never had so much food in his life. He was almost tempted to stuff a lot of it down his kaftan to save for later, but when he saw a few other children doing it, he thought it made them look messy. Her Highness had praised him when he'd been so neat and well put-together—and besides that, he couldn't imagine any of her kahyalar, like Lieutenant Çan, stuffing food into their clothes for later. He wanted to be just like them when he grew up, so he had to behave just like them. He stuffed his mouth until he felt sick, and that would have to do.

After the meal, they were led out in little groups of ten or fifteen. When it was Tadek's group's turn, the examiner led them all into a pretty room with sunshine coming through the windows—and there was her Highness, even more resplendent than she'd been at the Mint, all dripping with jewels, and a coronet on her head blazing in the sunshine and throwing rainbow specks of light everywhere when she moved. She was sitting on a throne with an armful of flowers—daisies, but the big beautiful kind that florists had in their shops, not the weak little kind that grew scraggly through the cobblestones in the summer—and beside her was one of the most ancient of the examiners that Tadek had spoken to that day, who had a stack of papers beside him.

The ancient examiner licked his fingers, picked up the top paper from the stack, peered at it, and then called a name, summoning up one of Tadek's group. Each time someone was called up, the examiner would speak to them briefly, and the child's shoulders would either slump or straighten, and the princess would smile and hand them a flower, and someone would come to lead them out through one of two doors.

"Tadek Hasira," said the ancient examiner. Tadek came forward and bowed deeply to her Highness, who caught his eye and smiled when he straightened. "Well done, young man," the examiner said in a quavering voice. He brandished the paper, which Tadek now saw was several papers. His *file*. "Not so often we see someone start out with glowing references." He leveled a stern look at Tadek, but he was wiry and lean and didn't remind Tadek of his father at all, so he didn't mind. "Make sure you live up to that promise."

For a moment, he didn't know whether he'd made it or not, and he almost asked. But then her Highness leaned forward with a *special* smile, one that was more real and personal than the ones she'd given anyone else, and she handed him a flower and whispered, "Well done, Tadek." And then someone came, and called him Cadet Hasira, and led him out through the good-news door.

The academy was wonderful. For the first year, he hardly had to work at all except at his studies, and they gave him three meals a day and a *real bed* with its own curtain around it for privacy in a dormitory with fifteen other boys. He got to bathe whenever he wanted, for *free*. He got to eat as much as he wanted, for *free*. He got to sleep, and he got to play with the other children, which hadn't happened much on the streets.

There was a day when he was rolling around in the grass outside the dormitory and laughing with one of his new friends when he lost the wrestling match and found himself pinned flat on his back. He looked up to the roofs and saw the banners of the kahyalar corps unfurl in the bright, fresh breeze, and his heart caught in his chest and unfurled just like that, and all the tension that he'd carried around with him for all his life went out of him in a sudden rush.

That's me, he thought, looking at the banner snapping in the wind. *That's me.*

7

Now

A few days passed. Tadek spent, oh, three or four hours a day with her. Sometimes he spoke. Sometimes he just stood there, either in front of her in parade rest or (feeling stupid as hell for it) by the door, as if he were on duty and appointed to her service.

He would have been wearing cobalt, then, as the rest of the core-guard did.

"How do I look in green?" he asked her one day, smoothing a hand down his kaftan. Knee-length green trimmed with black, for the colors of Şirya Manor. It was Kadou's smallest holding and his favorite, the one piece of fortune that his father had brought into his marriage to her Highness.

The first armsman's uniform that had been arranged for Tadek—either by Kadou or, more likely, someone in the great bureaucracy of the palace—had been nothing special. It had been equivalent in formality to something higher than a cadet of the academy but lower than a fringe-guard. A common uniform. A soldier's uniform. Nothing approaching the finely tailored splendor that his cobalts had been.

Kadou hadn't stood for that, of course. He'd arranged new uniforms for Tadek as swiftly as possible, each one masterfully made and of good fabric so he looked as sharp and dashing as he ever had in his cobalts. There were nine of them of varying formality—four in lightweight linen for the hottest days of summer, and two of light wool for cooler days, all appropriate for sparring practice or anything else that might require him to be rolling about in the dirt. Both the linens and wools were trimmed by a single band of black fabric around his bottom hem and his cuffs, yet they were elevated by the beautifully-carved wooden buttons and a hint of simple embroidery along the edges of the band.

Then there were the other three. First, the winter set, which was heavy wool partially lined in trimmed rabbit fur for warmth, plus a wonderful calf-length cloak—and rather than one band of black fabric at the hems, the winter set bore three decreasing bands of *sable fur*. Second, the low-formal set (appropriate for attending his Highness at most banquets and courtly events), made of mid-weight wool of excellent quality with shimmering black satin for the same three bands of trim and black buttons embroidered in green silk floss. Third, the high-formal set in emerald silk brocade. A simple brocade, yes, just a basketweave pattern, but Tadek had never owned anything so fine, and it was trimmed with black couching—silk cords sewn onto the fabric in twisting, intricate knotwork patterns, as if merely the brocade alone was not sufficiently fancy for his Highness's singular armsman. All three of the finer sets had been made with longer skirts in a fashionable cut that swung magnificently about Tadek's legs as he turned.

"He's kind of embarrassing when he decides someone belongs to him," Tadek explained to her. "Gets a bit carried away. You remember how he was with those toy kahyalar when he was little." Perhaps Tadek could wear his high-formal uniform to visit her once. It wouldn't see much use otherwise—it was only for the highest of state occasions. He probably wouldn't get to wear it until the idiots came clean about what they'd done (to wit: getting *married* and then haring off for their honeymoon without *telling anyone*) and her Majesty forced them to do the thing again properly.

Tadek sighed heavily at the very thought. *Doing it properly*, Usmim have mercy on him. Arranging a proper wedding would be weeks or months of work, and it'd all fall on poor old Tadek's head, wouldn't it. All the planning, all the micromanaging of Kadou's schedule—*and* Evemer's, because gods forbid that they try to assign Evemer his own set of kahyalar and his own personal secretary to manage his affairs. Tadek wouldn't stand for it. He would have a tantrum to Kadou about it. He could already envision the tedious struggle of establishing dominance over some uppity core-guard who thought they were *special*. They weren't. Tadek had been one and he knew that it didn't make you all that special. Just one of however fucking many there were.

Now, an armsman was special. An armsman *belonged* to a *person*.

So he'd arrange all the doing-it-properly, as her Majesty would undoubtedly demand, and after however many eons of work, there the two idiots would be in the temple, all gooey and soppy and shining-eyed at each other, and then Tadek—as if he hadn't done enough already to get them there, and with probably *no* appreciation for his efforts—would have to take a knee in his emerald silk brocade and swear armsman oaths to his new prince-consort.

Which he had not done yet.

The weight of that was beginning to nag at him in the back of his mind, a vague awareness of the *absence* of that oath, like a tooth that was just starting to wiggle loose.

But it was just the awareness. The need to *do it* was not itching at him—nor on them, he'd wager, because none of the three of them really felt like the marriage was really real yet, did they? Sure, it was real enough for the two idiots to go on a honeymoon, but they probably would have been having a sex vacation of one kind or another either way.

But it was *not* yet real enough for it to be time for Tadek to make his oaths to Evemer. Or (probably) for Evemer to want him to. Or for it to have occurred to Kadou that he ought to ensure his household was in order and everything was solidly nailed down where it should be.

No surprise there—Kadou was primarily occupied with getting himself, ah, solidly nailed down in an entirely different way. At some point he'd come out of the sex haze and realize there was someone else hanging around the place who had reasons to get on his knees for Evemer—really, the jokes were just too easy. If people hadn't wanted so many sex jokes about fealty, they wouldn't have made it involve so much kneeling, would they. Yes, that was the only reason Tadek hadn't sworn his armsman oaths to Evemer yet: Kadou was hogging the spot Tadek would need for it, and he was busy doing unspeakable things while he was down there.

Tadek couldn't tell her Highness about any of that. There were some things a mother didn't need to know, and some things he didn't care to speak aloud, for fear they might suddenly become more real than he was ready to face. For example: belonging to *their Highnesses* rather than to *his Highness.*

So all he said was, "I think I look nice in green. I hope you think so."

8

Then

Once a month or so, she came through the academy and greeted them, but it was ferociously hard to get attention or personal moments like what they'd shared on the steps of the Mint. Too many people crowding around, too many eyes watching like a hawk for any impropriety.

Tadek realized quite early on how closely they and their habits and behaviors were monitored. On a regular basis, the cadets got to speak to advisors, who talked to them about their academic achievements, goals, interests, and what they'd like to do to serve the royal family and the kingdom. In the second or third meeting, Tadek's advisor had referenced his file and earnestly said that she'd heard he'd had done marvelously well in a game of hide-and-seek with the other cadets the previous week when they'd been let out to play after classes, and she was curious what qualities made him so good at it.

It had been a bit startling that their game had been *noticed*—that his performance in it had been noticed. It stuck in his head in an odd way for some time, made him watchful in a way he hadn't been since he'd lived with his family, made him *careful* of how he behaved and what he revealed of himself.

So when her Highness visited the academy, he didn't run up to her and throw his arms around her like he wanted to and burble happily about how well he was doing in school. He stayed with the other cadets as they were brought before her, and he said, "Good morning, your Highness," in chorus with the others, and he was very polite and mannerly as she swept around and looked at what they were doing... And all the while he hoped and hoped and *hoped* for a smile that was just for him.

He got them, he thought. She always remembered *his* name, even when she had to ask other children to remind her of theirs again, or when she glossed over calling them by any name at all. And even when she couldn't stop to speak to him individually, when he was just one face in a crowd, he always felt like there was at least a moment of her eyes catching on him, *noticing* him, and a warmth that came to her face when she did. He held himself straighter and prouder for her, he did his best for her, and he hoped that she was happy with his work.

Sometimes, her Highness brought along Princess Zeliha, who was four years older than Tadek—eleven or twelve, taller than Tadek and wiry, and very fond (so he had heard) of horses and falconry and archery, and marvelously clever at all her lessons. She was always very polite to the cadets, but it was just the littlest bit stilted. She hadn't learned the art of her mother's easy warmth yet.

Sometimes, her Highness brought along Prince Kadou, who was a year younger than Tadek and just as painfully shy as he'd heard. On these days, rather than visiting the classrooms and seeing them at their work, her Highness came during their free time in the afternoons before supper when the cadets were permitted to play in a wide park beside the training fields. Her Highness's kahyalar would set up a pavilion for shade and a divan for lounging, and carpets to sit on, and she'd sit comfortably a little ways off from the cadets' games, reading a book or listening to a kahya playing music for her while Prince Kadou played by himself at her feet.

Tadek had overheard her telling her husband that she wanted to find playmates for Prince Kadou, so that must have been what the whole exercise was about: Putting him near other children his age and hoping that *something* would happen. Tadek watched out of the corner of his eye whenever they were there, and sometimes he saw her lean down to the prince—if he wasn't playing on the carpet with his toys, he was crammed firmly against her side on the divan—and whisper to him, sometimes even gesture towards the cadets at their games. He always shook his head, and she'd sigh a little to herself and sit back to occupy herself with whatever she'd brought.

Once, on a day Tadek knew that her Highness and Prince Kadou were likely to be in the park again, he endeavored to make sure everyone else was dead-set on setting up a wrestling competition after lessons, and then he brought along a ball and made a show of being very mournful and injured when no one was interested in playing with him. He played by himself, drifting closer and closer to the pavilion as he kicked his ball this way and that. Now and then, he eyed the prince, who was fully occupied with some little game of his own invention, involving a set of beautifully carved wooden soldiers painted with cobalt blue core-guard uniforms.

"Careful, cadet," said one of the kahyalar who was standing on guard scattered around the pavilion. Then, "Oh, Cadet Hasira."

"Hello, Lieutenant Çan," Tadek said. "I'm just playing kickball."

"I see. Mind where you're aiming," Çan said with a warm smile.

"I am!"

"At ease, Çan," her Highness said from the pavilion. "He's not the sort to get rowdy and careless." She met his eyes when he looked over, his heart lifting into his throat, and she smiled at him over the edge of her book. "No one to play with you, Cadet Hasira?"

"No, your Highness," he said, bowing to her immediately.

"What a shame." She glanced down at Prince Kadou expectantly. He appeared to have taken no notice whatsoever. "Kadouçiğim, sweetheart, do you want to play kickball with Cadet Hasira?"

The prince looked dubiously up from his toys at Tadek's ball. "No thank you, mama," he said, clearly a rote phrase, and returned to his own game.

"Maybe you'd like to invite him to come in and play with your toys, then?"

The prince froze and looked up at his mother with huge eyes. "No thank you, mama?" he said uncertainly.

"But it's *nice* to share, Kadouçiğim," she said encouragingly.

That seemed to strike exactly the wrong note, because the prince immediately snatched up his carved kahyalar, clutched them to his chest, and scrambled behind the divan and out of sight. "No thank you, mama," he said firmly. "I don't want to."

Her Highness craned over the back of the divan. "Why, love? He'll be gentle with them. He's a nice boy."

There was a long pause, and then a rustle and a clatter of wood, and a little hand dropped one of the kahyalar over the back of the divan into her Highness's lap. "He can play with Maral Mergen. I don't like her as much."

"Kadou," her Highness sighed, and craned further over the back of the divan. "What if you played *together*? You could play with Asanbughaa and he could play with Beydamur—"

"*No,*" the prince said, so audibly aghast that a few of the kahyalar around Tadek bit back smiles. "I mean *no thank you, mama.*"

Her Highness sighed again and turned back to Tadek with an apologetic shrug and a warm, rueful smile.

"Better luck next time," Çan murmured, patting Tadek on the shoulder. "We tried, though."

"Maybe Çan would like to play kickball with Cadet Hasira," her Highness said brightly. "And they'll have *so much fun.*"

"So much fun," Çan said immediately. "That sounds great."

Tadek was only a heartbeat behind on catching her Highness's drift, and he added swiftly, "Yes, so much fun. The most fun anyone has ever had."

"Wow," said her Highness cheerfully. "Isn't that nice, Kadou? Çan and Cadet Hasira are going to play kickball. Do you want to come help me keep score?"

"No thank you, mama," the prince said idly, clearly caught up in his own game again. "I don't like kickball."

Her Highness shook her head and returned to her book with an expression of carefully controlled exasperation.

Tadek looked up at Çan expectantly. "So are you allowed to play with me?"

"Yes, he is," her Highness said firmly, not looking up from her book. "He is in fact *ordered* to do it. Off you go, Çan."

9

Now

T adek wore his high-formal uniform to visit her.

"Look at this shit, ma'am," he said, holding his arms out and twisting his hips back and forth so the gorgeous fabric swung in pendulous luxury around his calves. "I look like I'm rich. I look like I'm in charge of something important." A few more swings. It was a bit hypnotic, really. "Well, I suppose I am already, eh? I'm in charge of looking after the lovebirds. They're fine. I had the morning shift today and brought breakfast to their room, and I was stupid enough to mention that most everybody else in the house had gone off to the village for the market, which resulted in me getting unceremoniously kicked out of the room so they could take advantage of not having to be quiet. So I'm wearing my high-formals as revenge, you see. Breaking it in now with you, somebody I *respect*, rather than at their inevitable second wedding." Swing, swing, swing. He walked back and forth in front of the portrait a little—he'd brought his crutch today, because he might have been overdoing it with the hours and hours of standing on his leg, and it would not have done for his muscles to seize up and tumble him to the ground when he was wearing his absolutely nicest clothes. He turned sharply at the end of each lap, the skirts of the kaftan flaring out magnificently. "Nice of his Highness to make sure I still look hot in uniform, isn't it? But then, when you have a lone, singular armsman, you don't want him wandering around looking mucky, do you? It would not reflect well upon you." Pace, pace, *turn*. "If you bother to dress your armsman up sharp as a tack, that says something about you, doesn't it?" Like that he was trustworthy—that Tadek had *his Highness's* trust. That Tadek was worthy, important—or at least important to his Highness. That he was beloved, that he belonged.

Kadou was a possessive little fuck, Tadek was *well* aware. As if the green and black wasn't enough, as if the word 'armsman' wasn't enough, even though no one else around had armsmen anymore—as if all that was not enough, he also had to make sure that Tadek *advertised* how extravagantly he was possessed.

Footsteps in the hall—Evemer's. A tap on the door; it opened before Tadek could decide whether to answer. Evemer stepped in, closed the door, and tucked his hands behind his back. Such obnoxiously perfect posture. It was if he had entirely eliminated his natural human inclination to relax and be at ease.

Tadek had seen him at ease just this morning when he'd brought breakfast in for them. He'd been cuddled up around his Highness, wearing nothing but a sheet over his lower half and twining a lock of Kadou's hair around his finger. He'd barely even glanced at Tadek when he'd come in, and really who could blame him, when he had the prettiest man in probably the entire world next to him, skin to skin?

Disgusting, lovesick fools. They deserved each other, and Tadek meant that as both a blessing and a condemnation.

"Good afternoon, your Highness," Tadek said, just to be as obnoxious as Evemer's perfect posture.

"Good afternoon, armsman," Evemer said, because apparently he was feeling a little bitchy today. Tadek turned back to the portrait. "I have been wondering something. Does Kadou know?"

"About what?"

"That his mother was. . . your lady."

"No." Tadek looked up at her. Who had been in the room with her as she'd been painted? Who had kept talking to her to make her eyes sparkle like that? Presumably either her husband or one of her kahyalar. "What's there to say about it, anyway? It's not a nice kind of conversation to bring up." Tadek felt a lump come into his throat and swallowed it down. "He's an orphan, Evemer, one doesn't bring up the topic of *parents* to an orphan."

"And he's your liege lord," Evemer said. "He'd want to know this about you." Tadek didn't answer that. After a moment, Evemer added, softer but no less firm and assured, "He wouldn't begrudge you this."

"No, he probably wouldn't." Tadek swallowed down another lump. "It doesn't matter, though. I wouldn't know how to bring it up." He rallied himself and managed to half turn over his shoulder to cast a skeptical look at Evemer. "Why are you trying to spoil your honeymoon with maudlin conversations, anyway? Where is he? Eating?"

"Yes," said Evemer, with the barest *shadow* of a *hint* of a smug quirk to the corner of his mouth—clearly a man who had gotten his dick wet and was pleased about it.

Tadek snorted and turned back to the painting, but couldn't resist. "How was breakfast? Sufficient rations to last the morning?"

"Nearly."

Well then. Tadek made a mental note to himself—if he wanted to avoid these absurd conversations with Evemer, he'd just make sure to haul in a mountain of food that *nobody* could get through in a day, and then Kadou wouldn't have to get dressed and leave the bedroom to eat, which meant Evemer would stay glued to him, wrapped around him and twining Kadou's hair around his finger rather than coming into Tadek's sitting room to interrogate him.

When Tadek didn't answer, Evemer said, "Why are you in your high-formals?"

"I wanted to show them to her."

He thought that was a simple, straightforward, obvious answer, but Evemer sighed as if he was being irritatingly obtuse. "He should know."

"Is that a command, your Highness?"

"Not yet," Evemer said with an edge of crisp threat. "Would it help if it were?"

Tadek closed his eyes and swallowed the lump down again. "Go back to your husband. Neither of you needs to concern yourself with this."

It was a long, long moment before he heard the door open, close again, and footsteps away down the hall. He felt the weight of Evemer's glare against the back of his neck for nearly a quarter of an hour after he'd gone.

10

Then

The fireworks for Princess Zeliha's eleventh birthday (and Tadek's eighth) were particularly astonishing, because that year he got to see them going off *right above his head*. They were set off from the training grounds, and everyone in the palace piled out into the Silver and Copper Courts to watch, or climbed up onto the palace walls and the rooftops of the dormitories and barracks. The fireworks were huge and bright, and they smelled of fire and sulfur and strange alchemical admixtures, and Tadek was torn between watching them in the sky and watching his own hands and arms turn bright pretty colors in the vibrant light each firework cast—blue or red, silver or gold, green and purple.

He knew they were for her, but her Highness had said that Princess Zeliha wouldn't mind sharing, so Tadek watched all the fireworks and picked just one that he decided was his—a burst of greeny-gold that dissolved into sparkling cascades like the hanging branches of a willow tree. It was the prettiest of them, but he was allowed the prettiest if he was picking just one, wasn't he? Princess Zeliha had all the dozens and dozens of other ones.

So then he was eight, and it was his second year at the academy. Now, in addition to schooling, his superiors began giving him little jobs to do—carrying messages thither and yon about the palace, sorting rice and flour in the kitchens, setting and clearing the tables in the mess halls of the academy dormitories or the kahyalar's barracks, or carrying out bowls and platters of food at mealtimes.

He liked it. He enjoyed school, but he'd begun to feel a little stifled and bored. The jobs gave him something to *do* and the opportunity to go places that he normally had no business being in, to meet people he would otherwise have never encountered, to stick his nose into places it probably didn't belong, and to work off some of his excess energy. Over a few months, he built up a mental map of the palace just as detailed as the one he'd had for the entire city sprawled below the palace plateau, or nearly so. There were still a few areas that were foggy—he'd never been *inside* the Gold Court, the innermost of the three areas of the palace complex, but he'd walked on the walls separating it from the Silver Court when he was carrying messages to some of the kahyalar appointed to watch shifts up there, and he'd looked out over the beautiful expanse of gardens and elegant residences, and he'd been struck nearly to tears by how calm, tranquil, and serene it was. He'd thought that it might as well have been a paradise. *I want to go there,* he'd thought. *I want to walk in the gardens every day.*

And he wanted to explore. He wanted nowhere in the palace to be off-limits to him. He wanted to walk every inch of it until he *owned* it, the way he'd walked every street in Kasaba City and owned that too. He wanted to be one of her Highness's core-guard. He wanted to stand guard shifts with Çan and the others.

A plan arose in his mind.

The problem was scheduling. He needed to run into her Highness's retinue at a time when he wasn't too busy and had an hour or so to spare. He took to signing up for extra messenger shifts, because those were the ones that took him all over the palace. Towards the end of his shift, he'd frequently take just one more message, rather than cutting off early when he knew that making it to the other end of the palace would take him longer than he was technically scheduled for.

It paid off, eventually. One day when he was on messenger duty, that last note he always took brought him to the door of a big office in the Ministry of Diplomacy, where Lieutenant Çan and Lieutenant Beyza were on guard outside the door—which meant her Highness was inside!

Tadek scampered up with a bright smile. "Hello, Lieutenant Beyza! This is for the meeting, I think." He handed her the message, all folded up and sealed with wax and the stamp of the Ministry of Trade.

Beyza skimmed the front with the label for which minister it was for and nodded briskly. "Good guess, kid, I'll pass it on." She leaned her spear against the wall, tapped softly on the door, waited for the call, and went in.

Tadek turned his smile onto Çan, who smiled back at him. "Hello, lieutenant. How's your shift going?"

"Quite well, thank you, Cadet Hasira."

"I was wondering something." Tadek said, scuffling his feet a little and making his eyes very big. "I'm done with my work for today so. . . Will you teach me to stand like that?"

Çan's warm smile broadened. "Like you're on guard?" Tadek nodded. Çan glanced up and down the hall briefly and said, "I don't see why not. Let's wait until Lieutenant Beyza comes back out, so that there's someone paying attention to the hall, hm?"

"Good idea," Tadek said, and shuffled up next to him with his back to the wall. He eyed Çan's stance carefully and mimicked it as best he could, with his feet shoulder width apart and his hands behind his back and his chin up. He didn't have a spear, so it wasn't quite the same, but he would try his best, just like he promised her Highness.

Out of the corner of his eye, Tadek saw Çan shaking with silent laughter, some two or three feet above his head, and Tadek took that to mean that he was doing rather well. The adults in the palace weren't like the adults down in the city—it was something magical about the white cadet uniforms, maybe. As long as you were trying hard to learn, none of the adults laughed in a mean way. Tadek had discovered that. And besides, Çan was always nice. He wouldn't laugh at Tadek—well, unless Tadek did something endearing or told a good joke.

It was only a moment or two until Beyza stepped back out and took her post at the opposite side of the door. Çan relaxed out of parade rest and murmured, "I'm teaching the youth, Beyza, if you wouldn't mind watching the hall for a moment." Beyza chuckled under her breath and nodded. Çan looked down at Tadek with another warm smile. "You're doing quite well. Your chin doesn't need to come up that high. Relax your back a little, or you'll be sore as hell after just a minute or two. Feet and hands are good. Ah, don't throw your chest out that far, just roll your shoulders back. There, good. Look at that, you're a natural."

Tadek beamed, but kept his eyes very properly straight ahead. "Thank you, Lieutenant," he said solemnly. "Can I stand watch with you for a little while? As practice?"

"Practice," Beyza whispered as if overcome. "Oh, he's cute."

"Certainly," Çan said, patting him on the shoulder. "It's good to practice."

"I'm going to practice a lot," Tadek said confidently. "I want to be a core-guard one day."

"You have to work really hard to be a core-guard," said Çan. "You have to study a little bit of everything, so that no matter what your charge requires, you can provide it. Not just guarding and fighting, but cooking and cleaning and dressing and tailoring and the rules of etiquette."

"And music and dancing and pleasant conversation," added Beyza. "And horsemanship. And excellent handwriting. And languages. And general good sense."

"Wow," Tadek said. That was a lot of things. "You know *all* that?"

They both paused. "Well," said Beyza. "Most of it?"

"Nobody needs to know *all* of it," Çan said. "Because everybody you'd be guarding would have more than one kahya. So knowing a little bit about a lot of things is good, but knowing a lot about a few things can also be good. Then there's overlap to cover all the basics, and a variety of different areas of expertise."

That was more like it. Tadek nodded. "I can do that. Let's pay attention now, we probably aren't supposed to be talking on shift."

"Baby kahya," Çan whispered to Beyza, clearly not meant for Tadek to overhear—but he did, and he glowed with pleasure.

Princess Zeliha's birthday fireworks—and his—came again. Tadek was *nine*, and he felt very grown-up and proud to be so close to ten—ten! Double digits! Only a year left, and then he and the other newly-ten cadets would be allowed to do all sorts of new, interesting things, like going into the Gold Court to deliver clean laundry to the residences, and setting tables for the royal family's dinners under the supervision of the etiquette masters, and even serving at banquets if they proved themselves to be very, *very* good. Tadek was going to be very good. All his teachers said that he was. He'd gotten excellent grades on all his schoolwork, and he'd advanced through his classes faster than most of the other children of his first-year cohort.

His teachers and academic advisors had continued to ask him what he wanted to be and what track of studies he wanted to follow. He always said core-guard, and the instructors always smiled kindly at him and said it was good to keep a few different options in mind, and had he considered the Ministry of Intelligence as a possible future?

The Ministry of Intelligence were spies. He knew that. He supposed that spies did a lot of the things that he liked—running all over the place, seeing things, meeting people, having nowhere that was off-limits, sticking their noses into things that weren't their business, walking every path until everything belonged to them. The whole world, even.

He wasn't really interested in the whole world. A bit curious, maybe, but when the other option was the Gold Court, the fireworks overhead on his (and Princess Zeliha's) birthday, the flag of the Mahisti dynasty flapping in the wind and even bluer than the sky itself. . .

Her Highness had said of her husband that he was a *country boy*. That wasn't Tadek. He was a city boy through and through. He'd been born in Kasaba City within sight of the palace, and he didn't particularly want to leave. Maybe once or twice, just to see what was outside of it, but *this* was his place. This was what belonged to him. The city, the palace, and one day the Gold Court.

Home, he thought idly, looking up at the fireworks on his ninth birthday. Home.

He hadn't been back to his father's house since he'd joined the academy. He hadn't written to them; they hadn't written to him. He didn't think they had ever come up to the palace to try to see him, either. They were probably glad to be rid of him—the *cockroach;* hah, he'd shown them, hadn't he—and he felt very little about being rid of them. They weren't his family, not really. His father was just the person who had sired him. His stepmother was just the person his father had married after Tadek's mother had died. His half-sisters were just two children that they had. Of that entire list, one of those people had been half of what had produced Tadek, and that was all.

He'd found more of a family here in the palace than he'd ever had down there in the city. He was fed here, far more than charity bread and charity rations. He was given clothes—pretty, clean cadet whites which showed every smudge and gave them plenty of opportunity to learn how to do laundry efficiently and thoroughly—and he was allowed to bathe as much and as often as he liked, and the instructors in the academy were generally kind and fair, though some were sterner and gruffer than others. And then there were people like Lieutenant Çan, who always had patience enough to teach him something if Tadek caught him in a spare moment. And her Highness.

Her Highness.

She still came to the cadet gardens with Prince Kadou now and then—sometimes Princess Zeliha joined them, or Prince-Consort Arslan. Prince Kadou never played with the cadets, nor the children of the other nobles. He just sat there on the divan with his mother and read a book, or worked on his lessons from his tutors, or walked around by himself (followed by a couple of kahyalar at a respectful distance) thinking whatever thoughts he had of his own. Tadek wondered sometimes if he had any friends outside his family. Tadek had loads of friends—everyone he knew, practically, was a friend.

Prince Kadou was eight this year. His birthday was in the late fall when the first snap of cold whispered through the air. Tadek's and Princess Zeliha's was in the spring when all the world burst into flower and came alive. There were fireworks for Prince Kadou's birthday, but only some years. Tadek had heard that his Highness hadn't liked them when he was little. *Such a shy little thing*, people said.

Prince Kadou was still shy when he and his fencing tutor visited the academy. His fencing skills were too advanced for him to be able to get useful practice with the students of his own age and size. Unfortunately, most of the students of the right skill level—Tadek's current classmates—had hit a growth spurt, so *they* were suddenly too big and gangly for it to be a fair fight.

Which left only Tadek, small but sharp.

Tadek found himself shy too when they were ushered in front of each other with the wooden practice swords. The prince had enormous eyes, just the same as her Highness's eyes, and he looked a great deal like his father, just as everyone said, and he was quiet and solemn and very polite—though Tadek got the feeling that the prince would rather be anywhere else besides here. Tadek was not entirely sure how to be properly polite back—was he supposed to let the prince win? Would he get in trouble if he didn't?

He cast a panicked look up at his own fencing instructor, who gave him a bracing pat on his shoulder and said, "Just do your best, Cadet Hasira, and remember the rules of fair engagement. Make it an honorable fight and you needn't worry."

"Yes, ma'am," he whispered. And she was right: he needn't have worried, because Prince Kadou was much better than him. Came of having private tutors for everything, probably.

They were made to fight three rounds together. By the third, Tadek had gotten the measure of him and escaped from the maneuvers that had nailed him the first two times. He was faster than the prince, and nimbler, and there might have been a couple of moments where he did something a *little* unconventional—not that it worked. Tadek tried to tire the prince out, made him *move*, made him lunge and run and change direction, harried him to where he *should* have been falling over in exhaustion like all the others did. But Prince Kadou—breathing heavily, granted—*just kept going.* And going. And eventually, at last, Tadek lost the third round and crumpled to the dust in exhaustion and defeat, gasping, "Yield!"

The prince backed off immediately, lowering his sword and looking anxiously from Tadek to his own fencing master.

"Thank him for the match, your Highness," the man said gently. "And a compliment would be most gracious, because he did very well."

Prince Kadou nodded and gave Tadek a very proper and correct version of the bow that a victor offered the loser, regardless of rank. "Thank you for the match, Cadet Hasira. You're very fast and good at footwork."

Tadek clawed himself up from the dust and hurried to bow back in the correct manner of loser to victor. "Thank you, your Highness. It was an honor and—" Prince Kadou was nodding solemnly, almost a little sad, like this answer disappointed him somehow. . . "—and I had fun," Tadek added impulsively. He called up a grin as Prince Kadou blinked in surprise and his grave look flickered to a little shy pleasure and relief. Her Highness had said to her husband that she thought he would be gentle with the prince, and Tadek would sooner have thrown himself off the edge of the plateau than disappoint her. "You're really good. Will you teach me that thing you did in the first bout?"

Prince Kadou's quiet look of relief stuttered away. "Your fencing mistress probably knows it." He kicked his foot against the ground exactly once, turned sharply, and ran back to his own tutor.

Well. That had been a success overall, in Tadek's opinion.

II

Now

One of his Highness's kahyalar had come down with a wretched cold, so Tadek found himself taking the morning shift *and* afternoon shift, which rather cut into his time to visit her Highness, but. . . well. Duty was duty, wasn't it? And even after all these years, he didn't want to disappoint her.

He brought the idiots their breakfast and pointedly ignored the fact that *some* kind of weird subterfuge was happening under the sheets. Even though they *looked* like they were innocently snuggled up in bed together, Kadou was pink in the cheeks and having difficulty keeping a straight face, and Evemer looked a bit *intense* in the eyes, and they each seemed to be rushing Tadek back out of the room as quickly as possible without actually *saying,* "Get out, we're busy."

Harlots, the both of them.

He stood outside the door, tuned out the ensuing *noises*—he fucking hoped they were a bit more circumspect when anybody else was on the guard shift—and settled in for the long haul.

Around midmorning and to his total surprise, the door opened and they both walked out, fully dressed and presentable. He wondered how many tries it had taken them. "Good morning, Highness," he said.

Kadou smiled and looped his arm through Tadek's. "Let's go for a ride."

"Sounded like you'd already been for one."

Evemer whapped him on the back of the head, but Kadou only laughed and pulled Tadek away down the hall. "Come on. I've been neglecting my armsman. I've barely seen you except at meals."

"*Neglecting*—did honeybee put you up to this?" Tadek said, glancing back over his shoulder at Evemer, who was ambling along behind them.

"We mutually agreed it might be nice to socialize with other people," Kadou said airily. "And Melek was starting to give us some odd looks."

"What kind of odd looks?"

Kadou glanced back to Evemer, who answered: "Çe mentioned very tactfully to me that I seemed to be spending a lot of time *alone with his Highness.*"

Tadek barked a laugh. "Not an inaccurate assessment of the situation. What did you say?"

"The way I overheard it, there was a long and pointed silence while, presumably, he stared çem down," Kadou said, grinning. "And then said something reproachful and haughty about duty and service being an honor that we should all aspire to fulfill with the best of ourselves."

"Right, right, *The Ten Pillars of War*, Admonishments to a Would-be Righteous Man—what is that, a paraphrase of number sixteen?"

"*Twelve*," Evemer said crisply.

Tadek snickered. "And poor Melek thought better of the gossip çe had smelled and was delicately angling towards? Changed the subject?"

"Left the room immediately," Kadou said merrily. "Poor Melek. I suppose if the kahyalar had all been gossiping in the kitchen about it, you would have let us know." Tadek had not been spending much time in the kitchen or with the other kahyalar, so he hadn't the faintest idea. He suppressed a wince—he *ought* to know these things, but it meant spending a great deal of time away from her Highness's portrait...

"So you're being sociable with little old me as a *cover*, then, eh?" Kadou squeezed his arm and gave him a limpid, beseeching look. Tadek rolled his eyes. They probably *liked* it this way, the perverts. No other reason to keep up the pretense—it'd be easier to just come clean and let the household realize that they were fucking, at least. Then they wouldn't have to sneak around, and they could be as noisy as they wanted without waiting for everyone to be out of the house or for Tadek to be on watch. It wasn't like anyone in the household would *care*, except for the incredible gossip value. All that'd happen here was that Evemer would get some hearty back-claps of congratulations and a good bit of teasing from a few of the others. *Attaboy, Hoşkadem, attending to* all *his Highness's needs, eh? Duty is such a heavy burden, isn't it? And service is an honor we should definitely aspire to fulfill with the best of ourselves, if you know what I mean, wink wink.*

"It's a cover *and* it's spending time with my armsman," Kadou said, still with that little pout. "It can be two things, Tadek."

"As you say, your Highness."

"So what have you been occupying yourself with? Where have you been?"

Tadek thought of the portrait in that study and swallowed hard. "Around," he said lightly. "Poking my nose into all the rooms, making a nuisance of myself. Picking flowers and thinking."

Kadou smiled. "That sounds nice. Oh, shall we take a picnic and ride up the mountain? There's a secret hot spring up there."

"Certainly, Highness, that sounds like an excellent plan." Especially the picnic, which would be helpful after the perverts made eye contact for too long and told Tadek to stand guard outside the hot spring while they did unspeakable things to each other. Tadek decided not to bring this up. Kadou would deny it—he was socializing with other people, he was trying not to neglect his armsman, et cetera and so forth—and Evemer would agree with whatever Kadou's assertions were, and they'd both sincerely believe that they definitely weren't going to change their minds, and then they'd be halfway up the mountain without a bottle of oil or *anything*. . .

Of course these things would all end up being Tadek's job to look after, in the end. Civilization itself would probably fall apart without him.

As they tied up the horses at a good spot near where Kadou said the hot spring was, Tadek said suddenly, with no earthly idea of what possessed him to ask, "Do either of you remember Lieutenant Çan?"

No, that was a lie. He had every idea what possessed him to ask. It was Evemer's glare on the back of his neck when he'd evaded Kadou's question about where he'd been and what he'd been up to. It was the exchange from the day before—*He'd want to know this about you*—and Tadek's own inability to start directly with the difficult topic of. . . *her.*

He couldn't start there. He couldn't just turn to Kadou and say, *Hey, you know how you never forget your first? Your mother was my lady and I have never stopped grieving her.*

So. Start sideways. Not *her,* but one of her kahyalar, who had died with her in that shipwreck.

The two answers came immediately and in perfect unison: "Vaguely," from Evemer and "Yes," from Kadou. "Why do you ask?" Kadou added, taking Tadek's arm again.

"Just thought of him the other day," Tadek said vaguely. "Good man."

"Yes, he—" Mystifyingly, Kadou cut himself off, touched his fingers to his mouth, blushed, and *laughed.*

"What?" said Tadek suspiciously.

"Just one of those memories that you don't think of for years and years, and then it hits you out of nowhere and, ah. . . gives you a moment of perspective on yourself." Kadou was still pink in the cheeks, his eyes dancing *so exactly like hers* that it made Tadek's heart twist. "Lieutenant Çan was my first crush."

Evemer made a small noise of, presumably, jealous outrage, and Kadou laughed again and turned back to him. "Don't be like that! I was *six!*"

Tadek ambled onwards. "He was pretty hot, I'll grant you—*ah.* Nope, I got it. Your Highness, you *predictable little shit.*"

Kadou covered his face, his shoulders shaking. "Leave me alone."

"You have a *type.* Hot, beefy kahyalar with shoulders to die for." Kadou groaned into his hands, still laughing, and Tadek decided to have mercy on him. He took Kadou's arm and nudged him to keep walking on the path Kadou had indicated. "Six years old with a little baby crush on a kahya is very cute of you, though. Was it a secret crush?"

"Gods, no, that's the worst part." Kadou touched his fingers to his lips again, biting back a grin. "I decided I was going to marry him when I grew up, so I told my parents, *and* Eozena, *and* him—" Tadek spluttered around a yelp of mirth. "And then," Kadou continued, as if very long suffering, "once my mother finished giggling, she said I had great taste in men—" Tadek's heart lurched a little, but not enough to halt his laughter, "—and that if she weren't married to Papa, she might think about marrying Lieutenant Çan herself. I got *so mad at her.* I tried to tell her that she couldn't, because I'd called dibs."

Through his own giggling, Tadek managed to wheeze at Evemer, "He's always been a possessive little shit about his kahyalar, you see."

"And then," Kadou continued relentlessly, gazing off into the distance with an admirable attempt at a noble expression, "I went over to Lieutenant Çan at the door, who was blushing like mad about what Mama had said, and I tugged on the hem of his kaftan and said we were going to get married. He was *very* sweet and tactful about it."

"Didn't want to hurt your *tiny baby feelings!*"

"He managed to keep a straight face even though my mother and Eozena were cackling like hens across the room. He very seriously said thank you and asked if he could have some time to consider it. And I said, *how long?* And he still managed to keep a straight face and said, *Maybe fifteen to twenty years, minimum,* and I said that was a long time, and he. . ." Kadou's solemn tone fractured into hilarity, "He said he just liked to really take his time thinking things over."

"And thus, you imprinted on your type," Tadek gurgled, wiping tears of laughter out of his eyes. "Hot, beefy kahyalar with shoulders to die for, who can keep a straight face, and who need a lot of time to think things over."

"Well," Kadou said philosophically, spreading his hands. "The heart wants what the heart wants."

"Hmph," said Evemer from behind them as Tadek managed to compose himself. He'd crossed his arms, but he was looking vastly mollified.

"He wasn't exactly like Evemer, though," Kadou said, smiling back over his shoulder at his husband. "He was a bit like you too, Tadek. Funny. Warm. He joked with Mama a lot, I remember that. They were friends, I think."

That tracked with what Tadek had known of both of them. He wasn't quite sure what to say, and they'd brushed up against the topic of *her* far more quickly than he'd been prepared for—

"Look at you, achieving all your dreams," Tadek crooned at him. "Marrying a beefcake kahya just like you always said you would—"

"Oh, hush. I was *six,* I didn't know what I was saying!"

"No, no, of course, just you and your little type—is that why you wouldn't play with me and the other cadets when we were children? Did you have crushes on all of us? Did you go around crushing on every kahya you saw—"

"Absolutely not!"

"Just the ones with good shoulders," Tadek stage-whispered to no one in particular.

R eaching the hot spring was a little adventure. It was only accessible by pushing aside some bushes, dropping mostly *down* through the alarmingly narrow opening of small rocky cave and clambering through a passageway—difficult with Tadek's leg in the state it was, but not impossible, and Evemer helped him when the ceiling was too low to use his crutch. The cave wasn't so long and twisty that it ever became pitch dark, and sooner than Tadek expected, the passage broadened out into a space the size of the large main room in Kadou's residence at the palace. It was mostly open to the sky and partially overhung with great slabs of boulders, and Tadek limped around the edge of the spring with his crutch, shading his eyes and peering up at the opening. "Why can't you access it from up there with a ladder?"

"It's much harder to get up there. Too many crags and little cliffs and steep rubble slopes," Kadou said. "You'd have to bring ropes and pulleys and such, so it's just easier to come in through the cave—oh, hello, love." Evemer had come up and wound his arms around Kadou's waist. He tucked his face against Kadou's hair and said something that Tadek didn't care to hear. (He did care, because he was insufferably nosy. Could he help it? He'd been trained as a kahya and, for a time, considered for a potential position as field agent for the Ministry of Intelligence, so you might as well ask a fish not to swim.)

Kadou's breath caught. "Oh. Right now?" Evemer nodded. "Hah. Ah. But—what about socializing with other people?"

"Shall I wait outside?" Tadek said brightly, going back towards the entrance with his best attempt at a bounce in his step.

"I thought we weren't going to neglect our armsman—" said Kadou, at the same moment that Evemer said, "Yes, thanks," and nosed closer to his neck.

Well, so they were both possessive little fucks. Good for them. It was practically Kadou's *job* to be possessive, and Evemer was permitted a little moment of hilariously irrational jealousy once in a while.

Tadek fetched out the bottle of oil from the pack he'd brought, placed it conspicuously on a nearby rock without looking at anyone, and waltzed out. Truly, civilization would fall without him.

"Y ou should tell him," Evemer said when they got back to the stables. Kadou had gone inside just ahead of them with his hair pulled over one shoulder to hide the love-bite Evemer had left on his neck. "He'd want to know."

"Leave it," Tadek said under his breath as they handed off the reins of their horses to the stablehand. "It's not your business." Blatant hypocrisy, considering how much interest Tadek took in things that weren't his business—and Evemer had all that kahya training in nosiness too, after all.

"It is. You're his, and he's mine, and so by algebraic principles—"

"Fuck off," Tadek said briskly. "I'm off duty now."

He went to his lady.

It was enough, wasn't it, to take one step in the direction of talking about the past? They'd talked about Lieutenant Çan, and Kadou had mentioned his mother twice, and. . . that was enough. It didn't have to be done all at once, if it were going to be done.

Really, it didn't have to be done at all.

Tadek had very little faith that Evemer would leave it be.

12

Then

He turned ten, at *last*, and he was taken to the grand temple with the other cadets who were being awarded their first rank promotion and could now make their initial oaths of fealty. They were all thrumming with pride and excitement and nerves, scrubbed to death and groomed and primped. They had been given new shoes with the pointy toes like baby versions of the ones the ministers wore, as well as brand-new cadet whites, now with dogwood-blue sashes to indicate that they had achieved their first promotion and were now not just cadets, but cadet-*kahyalar*. Promotion and the oath-making wasn't allowed for anyone under ten, because those were still just little kids, practically *babies,* and the teachers said that little children couldn't make oaths. But being ten meant that your teachers thought you were old enough now to be more responsible and to know what you were really saying when you made the oaths. Everyone who had been in the academy for a couple of years already when they turned ten got a promotion almost automatically, and the ones who had joined up a little later got it when they completed a certain set of core lessons.

The cadets' oath-taking was a frequent enough occurrence that there wasn't an overwhelming amount of pomp and ritual around it—certainly nothing like the later merit exams for promotion to fringe-guard or ministry assignments, which happened once a year and included a great party the night before, for luck—but they were still sent off from the dormitories with a round of cheers from their classmates and their seniors, and there were a handful of temple aunts waiting for them on the steps to show them inside.

Three generations of Mahisti crowns waited for them: the sultan himself, a man on the cusp between middle age and his declining years; his heir, her Highness the Crown Princess Mihrişah; and *her* heir, the young Princess Zeliha.

The oaths for cadets were fairly short, and they had all been feverishly memorizing them for weeks. They stood in a long row, alphabetically by first name, which put Tadek right at the tail end of thirty or so. One by one, the head instructor of the academy called them forward, and they knelt—first to the sultan, and then to her Highness, and then to the young princess.

Tadek had thought it would feel like a thousand years before it was his turn, but somehow it went by shockingly fast, and he was almost startled to hear his name called.

He knelt to the sultan, and swore his fealty with all honesty, and the old man murmured his answer in return, and Tadek did truly feel himself bound by honor in that moment.

He longed in his heart to swear to her Highness third and last, because in fairy tales, that meant that something was the most important thing. But she was second, and so he knelt to her second, even though it felt imperfect in his heart. He laid his hands in hers, and looked up into her beautiful, dark, dark blue eyes, and said the words he was meant to say, and tried to tell her without any words but the ones he'd memorized that he meant it, he meant it, he meant it.

In the songs and stories and in the epic poems that they'd been assigned to read in the academy literature classes, much was made of the oaths of fealty, the relationship between liege and vassal, the weight of that promise and what it meant.

My lady, he thought to himself, because she was. She *was.* She was his, and he was hers, because she had seen him, and extended her hand in kindness, and lifted him out of his circumstances and given him a new life, a new purpose, a new direction, a new paradise to aspire towards, a code to live by—and now a vow of protection and a promise of a home and a hearth.

My lady, he thought as hard as he could. He hoped she could see it in his face, and hear it in his voice, and *know. . .*

She might have known. She must have heard something, because a little gloss of tears came into her eyes, and she gripped his hands back as tightly as he was gripping hers, and she spoke her part of the oath with solemnity and pride—*my kahya,* she might have been saying, but Tadek wasn't a kahya quite yet. Soon. So soon. Six or seven or eight years until he made it to fringe-guard, and then another six or seven or eight until he could hope for—*expect*—promotion to the core-guard.

It was a thousand years away and no time at all, and *she* would be there at the end of it, and he could serve her the way her other kahyalar did, and he could wear the cobalt with enough pride to burst out of his body.

He knelt, third, to Princess Zeliha, who looked as much like her mother as Prince Kadou did their father. He laid his hands in hers, and recited his oaths with as much sincerity as he had for her grandfather... But halfway through, a strange moment passed over him, and he felt a wrenching perspective shift as the impact of *passing time* occurred to him: One day he would be as old as Lieutenant Çan was now. One day Princess Zeliha would be as old as her mother was now. It was entirely possible that it might be *she* he served—or even Prince Kadou—and not their mother at all.

Her Highness only wished for him to do his best. If he were appointed to Princess Zeliha or Prince Kadou, then her Highness—who might well be her *Majesty* by then—would want him to serve them with all the same sincerity and honor and loyalty and faithfulness that he would have shown in his service to her. She was still his lady, but if his lady commanded him to the service of her children, then that was a charge he would accept with nothing but joy in his heart.

He heard a little firmness and ferocious determination come into his voice as he finished his oaths to Princess Zeliha, and he saw her blink down at him in surprise and curiosity, as if he'd offered her a challenge. Then she squeezed his hands just as her mother had, and answered with a grace and majesty that went far beyond her years.

She would be his sultan one day, and he could already see she would wear well the mantle of power and authority and strength. He was, after all, *very good* at people.

Tadek stepped into the Gold Court for the first time, the innermost of the three areas of the palace and the one reserved for the private residences of the royal family, the nobles and governors, and the foreign ambassadors. He had prepared himself to feel nothing in particular—to not be *different* than he had been before, to be disappointed that he was still the same Tadek that he'd been all his life.

But it did in fact feel different. As he crossed the physical threshold into that paradise he had glimpsed from atop the walls, he *did* feel like he was stepping into a new self.

New privileges meant new responsibilities and expectations. He was asked to work harder than he had in the three years prior, but he had worked harder than that before he'd come to the academy, so it didn't seem unfair. Besides, how was it *work* when he got to see new places, explore an exciting new territory, meet new people, and learn new things? And, of course, being sent on shifts in the Gold Court meant more opportunities to see her Highness. Now he could go wherever he liked, and when he was free from his duties for the day, he could track down Lieutenant Çan or whoever was on the door guard and post up beside them and get in some *practice*.

He didn't like people to see how hard he worked—it was a holdover from growing up with his birth family, probably. He wanted his instructors to think that he was naturally talented, that everything came easily to him, that they could set him any challenge and he would achieve it. And so he found secret, empty rooms to study in and pretended like he didn't have to read things more than once to remember them, and he waited until late at night when all the others in his dormitory were asleep to slip out into the hall and practice sword-forms very, very slowly in absolute silence, concentrating hard to *imagine* the weight and length of steel in his hand, because there was nowhere to hide a wooden practice sword, and they weren't allowed to remove them from the training fields anyway.

But he didn't mind being seen practicing with her Highness's core-guard, because it didn't look that much like practice. It just looked like. . . taking initiative. They liked that, the academy instructors and the superiors in the garrison. Initiative, and a statement of intent, as if Tadek was saying that he wanted this so badly that he was going to be a kahya on his own if that's what it took—and whether or not anyone gave him permission to do it.

So he made sure he was seen. He made sure he knew *everyone* in the palace, not just by face but by name. He made sure that everyone knew *him,* too—Cadet Hasira, who was always cheerful and merry and good-natured, who was talented yet never once haughty or a sore winner about it, who was well-liked, who was friendly and honorable and generous to his peers, who was always the first to volunteer to help out, or to step in and take over someone's shift if they were ill. He made sure to sign up for at least a little instruction in every topic the academy offered, and he made sure to speak to his teachers outside of class hours to ask intelligent questions so that they would remember him warmly.

It was a *lot* to keep track of, but he didn't worry about gulping it all down at once. Besides initiative, they liked to see *growth,* and he had twelve to sixteen years to work on that.

If there was one distraction, it was other people. He liked having friends, and he liked working together with his peers, but sometimes he'd look around and feel. . . *something.* Some vast and irresistible compulsion to be close to one of the others, except that it was never just *one.* It was whichever of his classmates was in front of him, or several at once, and often it was whoever was most smiling and friendly to him. Sometimes he went days and days just *fixated* on one of them and couldn't for the life of him figure out why he kept thinking about Cadet Nadira's shiny hair and pretty laugh, or how quickly Cadet Basur had been able to soothe that spooked horse and how he'd petted its velvet nose so gently, or how Cadet Evemer had slammed him into the dirt in last week's hand-to-hand combat lessons, or how Cadet Ava and Cadet Mahet sounded when they spoke Vintish during language lessons...

Absolutely mystifying.

About halfway through that year, the headmistress of the academy came to Tadek and said that her Highness was going on a royal progress to inspect Araşt's gold mines, and the chief of her retinue had requested five or six cadets to come along. The headmistress told Tadek that he had been working very hard and that he would be offered one of the spots if he wished it—but reminded him that it was an *assignment,* not a reward, and so he should expect to work even harder than he did at home, since he wouldn't have daily lessons to attend to.

Tadek nearly burst out of his skin with excitement and couldn't say yes fast enough.

It was a month of travel, just him and her Highness (and twenty core-guard, and forty-five fringe-guard, and seven kahya-cooks, and fifty other kahyalar of assorted service positions, and six ministers from Internal Affairs and Trade and the Mint, five other junior cadet-kahyalar besides Tadek, plus a senior cadet-kahya—a man in his forties who was an *expert* on grunt work—to oversee them).

That, finally, was the hardest Tadek had ever worked. Each night, they stayed at residences of the provincial governors or the handful of nobles who were left—only a few families had supported the Mahisti coup that had overthrown the previous dynasty nearly two hundred years before; those families had retained their holdings, and everyone else's lands had been seized by the crown. In between those scattered noble residences were the governors' palaces (much less grand than the royal palace) and the manor houses of local officials, who always looked strained and alarmed but *very* honored when the royal retinue descended en masse upon them.

If they were scheduled to travel onwards, then Tadek's day went like this: He awoke at dawn or just before, splashed water on his face, hurriedly threw on his cadet whites, stuffed a hot bun in his face (because the cooks woke up even earlier than the cadets did), and hurled himself into packing boxes of supplies, loading wagons, feeding horses and getting them saddled or hitched up, helping to serve breakfast to the ravening horde as they all awoke, taking breakfast to her Highness herself, and so on. Once they got on the road, there was little time to rest. He'd be in the cooks' wagon, helping to take inventory or awkwardly chopping up ingredients in preparation for the next meal when they stopped at midday; or he'd be in the laundry wagon, mending clothes or sorting things into piles to be washed when they stopped for the night; or he'd be running messages up and down the wagon train in the heat of the day until his pristine cadet whites were impossibly stained around the hems with road dust. At the midday break, he'd be occupied with serving food and cleaning dishes afterward, helping with repairs to any broken wagons or reshoeing any horse who had thrown one, or refilling their water supplies, or sprinting into the closest village to try to buy some necessary thing which had been lost or forgotten or overlooked, or helping to pack up everything again to get back on the road, and only *then* having the opportunity to hurriedly stuff some food into his face again. The afternoon was much the same. When they finally reached the next residence, the work still did not stop: There was unloading the wagons, setting up her Highness's bed—frame, mattresses, sheets, blankets, pillows and all—in whichever grand room the noble or governor had offered, assisting the cooks, doing as much of the laundry as they could get through, serving dinner, cleaning dishes again, polishing everyone's boots, wearily downing his third meal of the day, and then falling into bed in immensely satisfied exhaustion.

If they weren't traveling and were scheduled to stay for a day or two for one of the gold mine inspections and the assorted ceremonies around it, then Tadek would only be *slightly* less busy. He could usually eat with everyone else, but the laundry mountain by then was horrifically large, and it took all six of them and their overseer (and sometimes a few of the other kahyalar-of-service who had a spare moment) working flat out to get caught up on it. Then there were usually banquets that the governors had prepared for her Highness, so Tadek would scrub himself clean and dash to the kitchens to haul a serving platter onto his shoulder.

Her Highness was not unmerciful, of course. There were a couple of times, particularly towards the end of the month, where she showed up at the service end of the wagon train when they stopped for the midday meal, sat down merrily on the chair one of her kahyalar brought along, and told them that the core-guard could pitch in to help out for once while the kahyalar-of-service rested and put their feet up. Everyone took this in great good humor, and it was immensely funny to see the cobalts washing dishes in a millpond or a brook—and laughing and flicking water at each other just as Tadek and the cadets did—or cooking or taking up the mending.

Of course, they *were* core-guard, so they knew all those skills with competency if not excellence, and they acquit themselves admirably on every occasion.

On those days, her Highness talked to the kahyalar-of-service and made them smile and blush with her compliments on their work, and then she called the junior cadets to sit around at her feet while she told them stories, or talked to them about their studies, or listened to their jokes, or—on one delightful occasion—tucked up the skirts of her kaftan into her belt and played kickball with them until they were all sweaty and caked with dust.

Once, towards the end of the month, her Highness sent a message back to the service wagons asking for one of the cadets to come keep her company for a little while. "Missing her kids, I'd say," the senior cadet said sagely, reading the note. He regarded his charges speculatively, weighing each of them up.

"Please, can I?" said Tadek desperately. He missed her—and it had been so *long* since he'd gotten to have a proper conversation with her away from everyone else. It was the separation of their positions—a princess might speak to a mere street urchin however she chose, but she owed fairness to her cadets and kahyalar, and she wouldn't want to show favoritism that might interfere with Tadek's ability to prove himself and achieve whatever goals he set his sights on. "Please. Please, I've spoken to her Highness before, we get along, *please.*"

"Let him do it," said Cadet Mahet, looking a bit green around the gills. "I couldn't string two words together if I were talking to her Highness all by myself." The other cadets fervently agreed.

"Off you go, then," said the senior cadet, and Tadek slammed out of the wagon and sprinted up the wagon train. Lieutenant Çan, riding on his horse beside her Highness's carriage, laughed aloud when he saw Tadek running up. "Cadet Hasira, how did I know it'd be you?" He leaned down to let Tadek seize his arm and hauled him up into the royal carriage without even a pause.

And there was her Highness, sparkling and warm as if she were *truly* happy to see him, and Tadek's heart unfurled like a banner in the wind, like a blooming flower under the warmth of the sun. "Hello, Tadek. It's been a while, hasn't it? Have you been enjoying the journey?"

"Yes, your Highness," he said breathlessly. "I'm glad to talk to you. Um. How can I keep you company?"

"Do you know any card games?" she said, rummaging through a box of things on the seat beside her. "I'll teach you how to cheat."

"Cheat?" Tadek demanded, aghast. The instructors at the academy put so much stress on honor and duty and loyalty that he'd almost forgotten what it was like to be an occasional-pickpocket mostly concerned with looking out or himself and his own priorities. *Cheating* seemed to be a thing of that world, not the one that he had been working towards for all these years.

"Sure. A little sleight-of-hand is no bad thing for a young man to know. And you never know when something might be useful, do you? It's good to have a variety of skills."

And that was how Tadek learned to cheat at cards. He didn't dare tell anyone—the only one who knew was Çan, riding right beside the carriage and rolling his eyes from time to time.

13

Now

In the end, just as Tadek suspected, it was Evemer and his kahya-trained instincts to meddle and make everything to do with his lord (sorry, *husband*—not that Tadek thought Evemer saw much of a difference) his own business.

There he was, visiting her Highness, standing vigil in the middle of the room with his hands behind his back and the best posture that Lieutenant Çan had taught him and ignoring the ache in his leg. . . And then he heard footsteps in the hall again, and they were *not* Evemer's.

Kadou's. Lighter, gentler, a slightly shorter stride. Tadek closed his eyes. He knew the rhythms of the footsteps of almost everyone in the house. Kadou's. His Highness, his oathsworn liege, who had begged her Majesty to lay Tadek's life in his hands. . .

He would want to know this about you.

Tadek turned away from the painting briskly and occupied himself with the bookshelf. It was mostly agricultural tracts pertaining to the crops grown around this area, and Tadek swiftly prepared himself to tell a small lie about the level of his interest in such things, if his courage failed him.

Kadou tapped on the door—why? It was *his* house—opened it, and peeked around the edge. "Hello. Evemer said you'd probably be in here."

"Did he," said Tadek, turning politely toward the door and reflexively offering a formal salute—a kahya's salute, fist to his chest. He couldn't help it. She was watching.

Kadou blinked at him. Tadek almost *never* saluted to him in private, not since. . . well, not since the year before, when her Majesty had been pregnant and Kadou had been so worried about her, and Tadek had ran out of comforts to offer other than. . . physical pleasures. Distractions. Flirtations. A little fling, to keep Kadou's mind off of his troubles.

"Did you need me for something, Highness?" Tadek said. Still too formal, but he couldn't stop. He couldn't disappoint her, not right in front of her picture. He'd been too lax. He'd fallen into bad habits, he knew he had. He really ought to have been more like Evemer—or Çan, really. Straight-faced, always proper, graceful in service, obedient, humble. Not so full of himself that he started to let things slip.

Kadou frowned. "No, not really," he said slowly. He sounded confused. Well, Tadek's demeanor must be confusing. He lowered his eyes and kept his mouth shut. "Evemer thought you'd probably be in here. He said I should come talk to you, but he didn't say why."

"Ah, but he has a very strong opinion about *should,* doesn't he. Particularly compared to other people."

Kadou shut the door and leaned back against it. "Yes," he said, with a soft smile. "But he usually keeps me pointed in the right direction. So. Is there something to talk about?"

"Nothing you need to concern yourself with," Tadek said. "Nothing that affects. . . us." *Us.* Strange phrasing to use, but he wasn't sure how else to refer to the fact that he had sworn his armsman oaths, that his life was laid in Kadou's hands. Kadou and Evemer could get *divorced* if they wanted to and didn't mind facing the scandal, but Tadek? He was bound to Kadou's side until death.

Was it presumptuous to consider an armsman more permanent of a fixture by definition than a husband was? Well, perhaps. If they did ever divorce—they wouldn't, but if they did—then Evemer would simply go back to being a kahya, wouldn't he? Theoretically, anyway, though perhaps not in practice. But setting aside all the other factors of society and consequence. . . Marriage was temporary; fealty was forever.

Fealty even went *beyond* death. The proof: His lady's portrait was hanging right there above them, and he had never stopped grieving her.

"You're behaving strangely," Kadou said, soft and gentle. Almost tender. Tadek didn't deserve that. "Armsman, will you tell me?"

He swallowed. "Don't command it of me, Highness."

"Why?"

He couldn't lie. He had thought he might be able to, but. . . No. Not right in front of her. In any other room of the house, he could have called up a smile, or brushed it off with a wry comment, or made a joke, or changed the subject—pretended like the agricultural tracts on the bookshelf were remotely interesting to him. "It's my own burden."

Kadou didn't look convinced. "You are my armsman. You are mine, and your burdens are mine. Can't I help with it?"

"I'm afraid what you'll say," Tadek said, lowering his eyes. "I'm afraid of upsetting you."

"What, like I'm some Shahre dynasty lordling who will cut off your hands for telling me a piece of bad news?"

"No, not like that."

"Like what?"

"Like someone I care about protecting from grief," Tadek said, a little too sharp. He hadn't always had such a sharp tongue. That had come. . . after. After her death, after the world went dark, after those years of adolescence when suddenly everything had been so much *harder* and he'd found his soul scattered through with all those shards of broken glass.

"Saying it like that doesn't make me *less* worried, Tadek. What grief? Why?"

Fuck it.

Tadek jerked his head toward the fireplace. The mantelpiece, with its pile of wilted flowers and today's fresh one on top. The portrait, hanging above.

He couldn't bear to look at Kadou. He kept his eyes at the level of Kadou's hems and no higher. He watched Kadou turn; watched him step across the room. Saw him lift his hand, probably to the flowers.

"Did you leave these here?" Kadou said gently.

And still he could not lie. "Yes."

"For Mama?"

"Yes."

"That was kind of you."

Tadek could say nothing to that. He crossed his arms.

"Is this the grief?" Kadou said quietly. "This? Her?"

"Yes."

Kadou was as much of an idiot as his husband was—but only sometimes. Other times, particularly when it had to do with one of his people, he was appallingly perceptive. Tadek knew this about him, and he could almost hear Kadou putting the pieces together:

Evemer had told him Tadek would be in here, and Evemer had told him there was something they should talk about, and Tadek was being cagey, and Tadek had left flowers below her portrait, and Kadou hadn't seen him around the house much except when he was on duty or had been specifically summoned. . .

Kadou came over to him and tugged at Tadek's arms until he loosed them, and then Kadou took his hand and squeezed it. "Tadek," he said very quietly. "Why do we need to talk about my mother?"

"We don't."

"Evemer thinks we should. Does he know why?"

"Yes."

Kadou clucked his tongue and murmured, "Kahyalar are all gossips," which made Tadek snort and shrug in agreement. "You think I can't know, because it has to do with her, and she's my mother, and it will hurt me?"

"It's not about her."

"Who is it about, then? You? Is that why you said it was your own burden?" Kadou sighed and tugged at Tadek's sleeve, and somehow Tadek found himself sliding down the wall with his Highness, sitting on the rug beside him, tucked into a corner between the wall and the bookshelf with their shoulders pressed together and their hands laced between them. "If it helps, I don't really remember her very well. I was ten when she died. I have a few memories—the one I told you earlier today might be the strongest one. Other than that, I remember her laughing. I remember going out into the gardens with her sometimes, or her bringing me along on her errands to the Mint or the Shipbuilder's Guild. I remember she taught me how to cheat at cards."

Tadek gave a short laugh, more wetly than he would have liked. "Me too. She taught me during one of the royal progresses to the gold mines."

Kadou nudged him gently with his shoulder. "Will you tell me whatever you told Evemer? Please?"

There wasn't any escaping it. Tadek closed his eyes. Kadou leaned in, set his head on Tadek's shoulder, and Tadek couldn't help but tip his own head to the side to rest on Kadou's in turn. He swallowed hard. The words seemed to weigh a thousand pounds, but he lined them up on his tongue, braced himself, and. . . "She was my lady."

It took Kadou a few moments longer to parse it than it had taken Evemer. He squeezed Tadek's hand. "Oh."

"Sorry."

"Why?"

Tadek shook his head. "It's not my place."

"Oh, don't be like that. Since when have you cared about your place?"

"It comes and goes." He scrubbed the back of his free hand across his eyes. It had come when she'd lifted him up out of the gutter and gave him a purpose; it had gone when she'd died; it had come back a little when he'd been promoted to the core-guard, and then a little more when he'd been appointed to serve his Highness; it had wobbled when he'd been demoted from kahya to Kadou's armsman. . .

"Tadek," Kadou said.

"What do you want me to say? How am I supposed to say any of it to *you*, when she was *your* mother—"

"And she was *your* lady," Kadou said fiercely, raising his head from Tadek's shoulder.

Fuck. Kadou getting fierce was practically a guarantee that Tadek had already lost the argument, because Kadou was never fierce for his own sake, always for Tadek's or someone else who belonged to him. . .

"Everyone has a mother," Kadou said relentlessly. "And no one gets to *choose* their mother. But she was *your lady*—not everyone has that, and it's *always* a choice. Frankly, in my eye, that's the weightier thing."

"Don't be ridiculous."

"How many flowers are over there on the mantelpiece? Will I count them and find one for every day we've been here?" Kadou didn't even wait for him to answer, because he clearly already *knew* that he would. "You lost your own mother when you were young, didn't you? I remember you mentioning it—and your father remarried. Is he still alive? Your stepmother? Do you know?"

"I don't."

"And your mother? Do you leave flowers for her? Are you still *grieving* her?"

"No," Tadek said, the lump coming hard into his throat and his eyes burning. "No, I'm not."

"My parents died when I was ten. I miss them sometimes, and I wish that I'd had longer to know them, but I am past my grief for them." Kadou turned toward him and seized Tadek's other hand before he could scrub it across his face again. "Nearly sixteen years, Tadek—why didn't you say? Does *anyone* know besides me and Evemer?"

It took Tadek a moment to speak. "No."

"Did you swear oaths to her?"

"The cadet oaths. A few casual promises."

"I don't believe that. There were more than just a few, weren't there? And not just casual ones. She was *your lady*. What oaths did you give her, beyond the ones required of you?"

It took a moment before he could bear to answer. "None that she knew about."

"Oh, *Tadek*." But it wasn't reproachful, and it wasn't hurt, and it wasn't offended that Tadek had overstepped and laid claim on someone who didn't belong to him at all—and then Kadou drew his hands free, and got his arms around Tadek's shoulders, and hugged him tight and close.

Tadek didn't quite cry. He just snuffled the snot out of his nose while his eyes leaked hot tears onto Kadou's chest, and his hands kept clutching at Kadou's kaftan like it was the only solid thing in the room. In all the world, maybe.

14

Then

She died in late summer, her and her husband and all her kahyalar and all the remaining noble families of Araşt and their children.

She and her husband had attended a wedding between scions of two of the noble families that had been most loyal to the Mahisti ancestors, who had won the throne from the spiteful and miserly Shahre before them. Such loyalty could never be forgotten, so of course House Mahisti had to make an appearance. Alas that the young couple had wished to be married on a ship, out on the ocean. Alas that *something* had happened out there—no one ever did find out what. The weather had been fine, so that ruled out a storm. Had it been a stray sea serpent, lingering near the surface that long after the six weeks of their breeding season, which had torn the ship apart in rage? Had it been a problem with the ship itself that had caused it to break apart in a rogue wave? Had it been sabotage?

No one ever knew, except that the ship had gone out for the day, and only painted driftwood came back. Not even bodies.

Tadek had been studying in the attic of one of the dormitories, that day. He came down to find the superior officers handing out oxblood armbands for mourning. He went up to one, nervous and already scared, and tried—unwisely—for a joke, as if that would stop whatever terrible thing this was from happening. "Wow, who died?"

Her Highness. The Prince-Consort. All the nobles. Missing at sea, presumed dead.

A silent, devastating shockwave for the royal family, for the country, for Tadek.

He broke that day.

He had read in the epic poems and the stories that when someone was grieving, the sun went dark in their eyes. He had thought it a poetic fiction, but no—it really was as if a great light had gone out of the world. As if the air itself had been sucked away. He could see, but he couldn't see. He could breathe, but he couldn't breathe.

He wandered, stunned, through the Copper Court, with some inchoate hope to find someone, *someone* who would tell him it wasn't true. But everyone else was wandering too, just as stunned. The palace was dead silent. No one dared to speak above a whisper.

Someone said that the entire harbor had emptied, all the ships flying out to sea to search for survivors, and so Tadek waited by the gate for hours, long into the night, hoping that someone would come, that there would be word, that there would be a miraculous rescue. . .

No one came, except the dawn. He waited and waited and *waited,* and eventually someone told him that he should go and have something to eat. Later, he would numbly marvel to himself that he had no memory whatsoever of who had told him about the ships or sent him to eat—not their faces, nor their names, nor even whether it had been the same person or two separate people.

He was eleven years old, and he had lost the thing that mattered most to him in all the world. The earth had shaken under his feet; the glass in all the windows of his heart had shattered to dust; the sun had gone dark; there was no air. There was nothing left but devastation. Desolation. Cataclysm.

He drifted.

He drifted for a long, long time.

He was twelve. He drifted. He visited her portrait in the royal gallery from time to time, when he thought no one would notice, and felt utterly *crushed* by guilt.

He knew that he couldn't have done anything to protect her if he'd been there. Lieutenant Çan had been with her—if *he* hadn't been able to do anything, then what good would Tadek have been?

He knew that, but it didn't help. He was alive, and they were dead, and that didn't seem right or fair. He wanted to trade places and bring her back, even if it meant giving up his own life—the world would be *better* if he could. The world had been better with her in it. It didn't need Tadek like it needed her.

He was thirteen. He discovered kissing, and why he felt so mysteriously *compelled* by so many of his fellow cadets, and still he drifted.

He was fourteen. Quite a lot of people were discovering kissing. He drifted. He cultivated a personality that would camouflage the gaping, yawning hole in the center of his chest.

He was fifteen. He started to feel. . . a little less like he was drifting, but certainly not like he was anchored. He had kissed half of the other cadets his age, and fooled around with perhaps a dozen of them. It helped him feel like he was a little bit less alone, sometimes. Also it was fun, and it felt good. Very little felt really good these days, but that did.

He was sixteen. He was well-known by that point as the person who knew everyone—and the person who was always interested in some recreational kissing-well-maybe-just-a-bit-more if someone asked him.

In a wild and desperate act of self-sabotage, he flung himself at the fringe-guard exams as early as he was allowed. He was utterly *sure* that he would fail—on some level he *wanted* to fail. He wanted some other hurt, some other devastation which would overtake the huge empty place in the center of his chest where *she* should have been.

He was satisfied and disappointed in equal measures when the instructors said he'd passed and called him a prodigy, but he went to visit her portrait and tell her about it, and he went to the temple a few days later, wearing the sky-blue of his new fringe-guard uniform so he could swear his oaths anew to the sultan and Princess Zeliha, and his heart had cried out like a little lost kitten at the wrenching absence of *her*.

He was seventeen. He was anchorless.

He wondered, once, if he'd been a little bit in love with her, but the thought was instantly repulsive to him. Of course he had been, but not like *that*. Not in a way that anyone else would understand. It wasn't like the obsession his peers had with each other, or all his dozens of little infatuations and attractions and flings.

She had been his *lady*, like in the stories, and that was something entirely different—and infinitely more important, really.

He was eighteen, nineteen, twenty, twenty-one, twenty-two, twenty-three—

He was interviewed by a panel of his instructors, a few superior officers of the kahyalar corps, and one of the representatives of the Ministry of Intelligence. They talked to him once again about what he wanted to do and how he thought he could best use his talents in service of the crown.

"I'd like to take the core-guard exams," he said firmly. "I've only ever wanted the core-guard."

They knew that, of course. It was probably in his file, which had grown to a stack of documents more than two inches thick.

He took the exams. He passed, and at last, at *last* he was given his beautiful cobalts. The first day he had them, he wore them to the royal gallery to show her.

He had made his oaths to the sultan and Princess Zeliha earlier that day. His Majesty was looking very old, and Princess Zeliha very grown up—twenty-six, she was now, as strong and assured and gracious as anyone could ever have hoped for—and people in the garrison gossiped that his Majesty might abdicate and retire to a quiet country estate with his queen-consort, and let younger and more energetic hands take over the running of things. Princess Zeliha was ready for it, people said. She'd be good at it. And his Majesty was so tired these days. . .

Tadek had no care for all that. It should have been *his* lady next on the throne. He should have been in his cobalts to make his oaths to her as sultan, and he would have wept with the joy and honor of it, and served her with the very best of himself.

After the ceremony in the temple, he went to the royal gallery to visit her. There was no one else there, so he bowed as extravagantly and floridly as he could and held out his arms to show her his beautiful, *beautiful* new uniform, two shades off from perfect Mahisti ultramarine.

"I made it this far," he whispered to her. "I made it all this way."

He'd sworn his oaths to the sultan, to Princess Zeliha—and it felt only right for there to be a third, and for it to be her portrait. "I'll do my best," he said. "I promise. I'll protect Prince Zeliha and Prince Kadou with all my heart, with everything I am, with my *life*. I promise."

He was twenty-three, twenty-four, twenty-five—

Princess Zeliha was now *Sultan* Zeliha, and Tadek was appointed to Prince Kadou's service, and then he was in Prince Kadou's bed, kissing him until he gasped, fucking him until he forgot whatever terrors he'd thought up about her Majesty's pregnancy, pinning Kadou's hands down and *having* him as the prince's heels dug into his buttocks, having him until Kadou shook apart for an entirely different reason than those strange and illogical fits of fear that no one but Tadek knew about.

It helped Kadou; it helped Tadek. He was serving. He was useful. He was protecting the prince, and he *belonged*—and besides that, sex was *fun*. It felt good, and his Highness was the most beautiful person Tadek had ever seen in his entire life, to the point that it was almost strange to kiss him, as if he were a statue or a work of art that should have been unkissable. Also he fucked like a *mink*, which was a great bonus.

He was twenty-six—

15

Now

Kadou held him for a long time, stroking his back.

At length, Evemer's familiar footsteps came into the hall, and Tadek tried to pull away, out of Kadou's arms. Kadou kept firm hold of him. "No, Tadek. It's fine."

"He'll be *jealous*," Tadek snuffled, trying to wrestle himself free. "He pounced on you in the hot springs just because you were talking about your baby crush on Lieutenant Çan—"

"And if he dares to get snippy about me *comforting my grieving armsman*, I'm going to drag him out by his ear and give him a *very* stern talking-to about the obligations of fealty. But he won't, because he already knows it."

The knock on the door, and Kadou promptly said, "Come in."

Evemer came in, looked around, found them on the floor in what *Tadek* would have felt was a compromising position. He did not attack Tadek immediately, didn't drag him out to drown him under any water pumps, didn't do anything except give one mild nod, almost approving, as if something had been set right. He shut the door and joined them on the rug, his legs folded tailor-style and his hands on his knees. "He confessed?"

"Eventually," Kadou said. "Thank you for the heads-up, love."

Evemer shrugged a little. "It is our duty to care for him."

"See?" Kadou said pointedly, poking Tadek in the ribs. "He knows already."

Tadek muttered and managed to push himself off Kadou's chest and lever himself upright, wiping at his face with his cuffs. Kadou kept rubbing his back. "You're both making too much of a fuss."

"No," said Evemer, at the same moment Kadou said, "I disagree."

Kadou added to Evemer, "No one knows she was his lady except us."

"He hides the things that matter," Evemer replied, nodding.

Kadou leaned in and wrapped his arms around Tadek again. "Why didn't you tell anyone? Because it wasn't official, and you thought it wasn't your place?"

"Who would have believed me?" Tadek rasped.

"I believe you," Kadou said. "And Evemer believes the *hell* out of you. He was very, very firm that I should talk to you and get you to explain what was going on."

"If you have been loyal to her for fifteen years—" Evemer began.

"Twenty," Tadek said wetly, wiping his cheeks again.

Evemer paused. "You were *seven*?"

"She's the reason I'm *here*. She's the reason I joined the academy. She's—" His voice broke, and he could only look at the portrait and gesture. "It was *always* for her."

Kadou hugged him tighter. "Your lady," he said softly.

Twenty years of thinking those words in his most secret thoughts.

Twenty years of feeling it, following it, holding that ember close in his heart.

Twenty years of making promises to her and keeping as many of them as he could.

Twenty years of *believing* so hard in those words, and yet knowing that they weren't real—but here were his Highness and Evemer fucking Hoşkadem, who of all people in the world Tadek would have considered pretty acceptable authorities on how fealty was supposed to work. Here they were, and *both* of them had accepted it and instantly believed that it was as real as the earth under their feet, without any proof but Tadek's own word and the pile of wilting flowers on the mantelpiece. They *believed* him, as if Tadek wasn't just pretending or dreaming it up or lying, as if he *wasn't* presumptuous for choosing to swear himself secretly to her—

Well, maybe it was just that they knew something about making secret oaths to someone very important and it went against their obnoxiously rigid ethical code to be hypocrites in this regard.

"Can we do anything for you?" Kadou asked gently. "Is there any recognition you think you've earned for this?"

"I haven't earned shit," Tadek muttered.

"Not even for twenty years' steadfastness in silence, when no one expected it of you?" asked Evemer. Tadek glared at him.

"Or if not recognition, then something else?" Kadou pressed. "My grandparents' kahyalar are in their wills—and there's the grief pension—"

"I don't want *things* or *money*," Tadek snapped.

"Were you permitted to attend her funeral?"

"Everyone attended the state funeral."

"But you could have stood with the others at the. . . Oh." The *others*. He meant the other kahyalar who had been close enough to her to be sworn to her permanent service. Except there *hadn't* been any of them at the funeral except the now-Commander Eozena. All the rest of the household had died on the ship, doubtless trying until their last breath to protect their lady and their lord. "We could have a memorial, if you wanted to stand where you should have been permitted to stand."

Tadek shook his head. Too much fuss, and he was too used to it being a *private* thing.

"A token, maybe?" Kadou asked gently. "Something of hers you could carry with you? I have a lot of her jewelry, and Zeliha has the rest."

Tadek's eyes burned. "I'm used to those being yours and her Majesty's now. It wouldn't feel like hers." There was nothing he wanted—he hadn't *earned* anything, hadn't even really served her directly except for that one month on the royal progress.

After a long moment of desolate silence, Evemer stirred himself and said quietly, "Armsman."

Tadek sniffled and looked balefully over at him. Evemer paused, and Kadou lifted his head from Tadek's shoulder—and then Evemer shifted from comfortably cross-legged in front of them to a more formal posture on his knees, sitting on his heels, and he genuflected formally to. . . who the fuck was he bowing to? Kadou? Why?

Evemer did not rise from his deep bow as he spoke. "Armsman Hasira, you are the last alive who was close enough to Princess Mihrişah to call her your lady."

"What's he fucking doing," Tadek snapped. "What are you doing? Stop that."

Evemer still did not rise. "I would beg a boon."

"What? What do you want?"

"Her blessing to marry her son."

Tadek flailed to his feet, heedless of the screeching pain of his injury, and Kadou clapped his hands over his mouth with an incoherent squeak. "Fuck off! Get up! Stop that! Come out to the water spigot, Evemer, it's your turn to get pinned under it! What's *wrong* with you?"

Now Evemer sat up, and Tadek saw to his terror that he had that same fierce look that Kadou got sometimes. "This isn't a joke."

Tadek's eyes *burned*. For a moment, he was entirely speechless. "Why are you asking *me* for that? Go ask her Majesty!"

"But she was your lady."

"Fucking *gods!* So suddenly *I* have the authority to—to *give her blessing by proxy?*"

Evemer looked up at him, utterly serious, utterly patient. "She was your lady. You would know whether she would."

Tadek sank back onto the carpet, somehow both numb and a jumble of screaming, confused *feeling*.

Kadou, hands still clapped to his mouth, turned to him with his eyes shining—*her* eyes—gods, he looked like her when his face was like that, gods, they were her expressions. He had her hands too, so when he covered up half his face, with only his eyes and hands showing—

"Please," Kadou whispered. "Tadek. Would she?"

"She was your *mother,* you should *know*—or her Majesty would know—you can't ask *me*—"

"I'll ask her Majesty for her Majesty's blessing." Evemer said. "But not for Princess Mihrişah's. She was her Majesty's mother. She was *your* lady. So I'm asking you."

"Fucking hell—Eozena, then, go ask her!"

"She was Papa's," Kadou said faintly. "She called Mama 'Your Highness', but he was 'my lord.' I remember that."

Evemer nodded firmly. "I will also ask her for his blessing, when it is time. But I am asking you for her Highness's."

Kadou caught Tadek's hand, squeezing tight. "Tadek. Tadek, please, *would she give it?*"

Tadek looked back and forth between them, helpless, pinned against the wall like a butterfly. Fuckers. Fuckers, how could they take him this seriously? How could they believe him *even unto this*?

The awful thing was, it was straight out of one of the epics. Once, there had been *law codes* that would have given a greater weight and consideration to *Tadek's* word about his lady's wishes than to even the word of her children. You made vows—you chose someone, and they chose you—and you kept your promises faithfully, and you served as you were asked, and your service was returned with love and protection and belonging—hearth and home. And so in the epics, in the old law codes, the word of a faithful kahya meant more than the word of an heir.

He swallowed. His eyes burned. His lungs were tight, and there was not enough air in the room—he felt as if he were drowning, like all her other kahyalar who had drowned with her. This was what he got for not being willing to accept anything else—he wanted no money, no recognition, no tokens. So what did he get, when he refused all else? *Not a reward, but an assignment,* as his instructors had once told him.

Fuck.

"Of course she would have," he choked out. The words were surging up in his throat, and there was no hope of stopping them or filtering them or coming up with some way of saying them that would sound pretty in an epic poem later—was this how all the other faithful kahyalar had felt when they were called to testify on their liege's wishes when their liege was dead, or incapable, or ill? Was this the true reward of loyalty—trust and faith so profound it was faintly horrifying? "Fucker. Asshole. Evemer fucking Mahisti-eş, of *course* she would have given you her fucking blessing! Why do you have to ask me? She told Kadou he had good taste in men when he was *six*—she joked about how she might have married Lieutenant Çan herself! But none of that fucking *matters,* you absolute idiot, because he *loves* you and you make him happy and that's *all she would have fucking cared about—fuck, gods—*"

He buried his face in his hands as hot tears spilled over, and Kadou flung his arms around him again, hugging him tighter than ever.

16

Then

Her Majesty Sultan Zeliha stood over Tadek with the angriest expression he had ever seen on her face. It looked *wrong:* She looked so much like her mother, but her mother had never been so angry.

"What were you thinking, Lieutenant Hasira?" she snapped. "You attacked the father of my child. Two kahyalar are dead. Help me understand what happened."

He was numb with terror and relief—his Highness wasn't dead, he was safe, he was *safe,* he hadn't disappointed her—gods, he couldn't have lived with himself if Kadou had died on his watch. He would have had to kill himself like the kahyalar in all those old stories when they failed spectacularly in their duty and had broken oaths that they held as dearly as the ones Tadek still held to her late Highness, who would have been his lady. . . (*Who had been*, he thought sometimes when he was letting himself be maudlin.)

He had nothing to hold back from her Majesty. No reason to prevaricate or lie. He bowed his head and he told her everything—that his Highness had been afraid of Siranos, the father of her Majesty's newborn daughter; that Tadek had tried to find out if he were any threat, had asked around in the garrison, and had only been proud to know so many people were as loyal to his Highness and her Majesty as they should have been; that Tadek had truly, truly thought that his Highness might be in danger. . .

"You ought to be killed," Zeliha said, placing her hands on her desk and leaning across it towards him. "Do you understand? You ought to lose your life for this kind of carelessness—and if not executed, then you ought to be imprisoned. It is not *acceptable* to make mistakes costly enough to be paid in blood."

"I know," he said, broken, shattered, and scattered to the four corners of the earth. "I know."

She glared at him. "I will speak to my brother before I make any decisions."

She came back to him later. He'd been locked in a room that couldn't really be counted as a jail cell. Her face was drawn and stony, and she had a great stack of papers in her hands more than three inches thick.

"Tadek Hasira," she began formally. "You are hereby stripped of your titles and rejected from the kahyalar corps."

But not dead. That was something. Maybe. Maybe that was worse. He couldn't decide. "Thank you, your Majesty."

"I'm not done," she said sharply. "My brother the prince has entreated me for mercy. He has begged for your life to be laid in his hands. You will serve as his armsman, and all the responsibility for you henceforth will fall on his shoulders." Tadek was too numb for that to hit him immediately—it sank in slowly, achingly, like a dagger pushed almost gently into his heart. "If it had been just him, I would have been of a mind to overrule him and turn you loose. Exile, I was thinking, because why bother throwing you in a prison where we'd still have to pay to feed you? Luckily for you, someone else thought to defend you." She threw the papers on the floor in front of him—they spread out in a long river, a few of them scattering to the sides. "Good luck with your future endeavors, Armsman Hasira, and may the Lord of Trials never again test you so catastrophically."

And with that, she stalked out.

Tadek lowered himself to the floor as painstakingly as if he'd been seventy years older, and slowly picked up the papers.

It was his file. His records of everything since he'd joined the academy at age seven—his grades, the list of certifications he'd achieved and exams he'd passed, notes from his teachers on his behavior and personality, assessments of his aptitudes and some possible recommendations for how and where to assign him when he advanced for promotion. . .

And right at the end of the stack—which meant it was the first thing that had ever been put in his file—there was a note, written in an elegant hand on beautiful, expensive paper:

Tadek Hasira is seven years old; I have spoken to him on a couple of occasions, long enough to be confident that I have gotten the measure of him: If we treat him well, he will repay us tenfold. If we love him, he will be loyal forever. If we give him opportunities, he will rise to meet them and shine brighter than gold.

That said, something tells me that one day, he's going to make his first and greatest mistake, and by the time that it happens, he might have risen far enough and grown confident enough for that mistake to become a very big one.

For whoever reads through his file at that time: I recommend clemency, particularly if this great mistake has been his first real error and my aforesaid predictions of his loyalty have otherwise been proven beyond the shadow of a doubt.

Please, forgive him if you can. He has a good heart.

Signed and sealed by the hand of the Crown Princess, Mihrişah Mahisti, in the 179th year of our dynasty.

17

Now

The next day—the day after Tadek had confessed, after Evemer had asked that appalling question—his injured leg was horrifically sore. For once, he didn't much want to go up the stairs to stand his aching vigil before her portrait.

For once, he thought it might be alright if he. . . didn't. If he let himself rest from feeling those endless, rolling ocean waves of blue-black grief. If he forgave himself, just once, for being alive when she was not.

A week or two went by. One day, someone arrived at the manor. When Tadek ambled down to see what the commotion was, he overheard their visitor say, deeply nervous, that çe was a painter from a nearby town—not Şirya, but the next biggest one over—and that the prince had summoned çir.

Tadek didn't have much truck with painters or paintings beyond the ones of his lady, so he thought nothing of it, and was soon distracted when Evemer appeared out of nowhere and brusquely ordered Tadek to accompany him out to Şirya Village to fetch something that Kadou wanted. Tadek duly hobbled out with him to the stables, let Evemer help him clamber onto a horse once they were saddled, and off they went.

Tadek only got suspicious when Evemer kept coming up with *other, different* things that they had to hunt down. It was not Evemer's style. He would have had a perfect list of each item he wanted to acquire or task he wanted to complete, and he would have gone down the list in order, and then hurtled back along the road that ran beside the long black lake to the manor house where his beloved was *all alone* and tragically unfucked for, what was it now, six whole hours?

But first it was sweetbuns from the baker, and then it was some groceries and supplies for the manor, and then it was off to the farrier because Evemer thought his horse (a gorgeous blue-roan gelding that Kadou had seen in a field during the journey out to Şirya and had immediately bought from its owner and given to Evemer as a present; Tadek had had to make loud noises to the rest of the kahyalar about how it was just because Evemer had saved the prince's life and that was the sort of special treatment you got when you saved your lord's life, yep, that was the only thing, not unusual or remarkable at all; just like in the poems, really, when you thought about it) was having problems with one of its shoes, and then it was over to the butcher's to have them send up some marrow bones for roasting and stew with the next order, and then—

"What are we doing?" Tadek asked warily.

"Errands," Evemer said.

"Yes, but you keep coming up with new ones."

Evemer remained utterly impassive. "I have a list. We're nearly finished."

Tadek didn't quite believe him, but fine.

Then Evemer also had to visit the Şirya apple orchards because he, quote, *wanted to look at them*, at which point Tadek squinted at him and said, "Why are you keeping me out of the house?"

"That's a strange assumption," Evemer said.

"I'm going back, then. You don't need my help."

"Perhaps I wanted your company."

"Bullshit."

"Is it?"

Tadek spread his hands. "Honeybee, why would you want my company when you could be keeping much sweatier, nakeder company back at the house?"

That made Evemer go all misty and yearning in the eyes.

"Yes," Tadek said, gesturing enticingly in the direction of the manor. "The company back there is very sweaty and naked these days, isn't it? And willing. More than willing. *Eager.* Starved for your dick. Let's *go.*"

Pointless to go up against Evemer Hoşkadem when it came to a battle of wills. He straightened his shoulders and said firmly, "I have two more errands to do."

"You have two more lies," Tadek corrected. "Have fun with your lying. I'm going back. If your husband is naked and weeping about being *abandoned* and *neglected*, then I'm going to pet his hair and manfully let him cry on my shoulder and be very strong for him in his time of woe and suffering."

"No," Evemer said, leading them in towards a little farmhouse in the distance—presumably the home of whoever oversaw the orchards. "I require your attendance, Armsman Hasira."

"I feel like I don't really *have* to obey you. It's not official. I'm not going to be committing criminal insubordination. What kind of trouble am I going to get in if I don't?"

"You can find out, if you like."

"Maybe I like."

Evemer shrugged one shoulder. "Fine. Leave the prince-consort unattended on an open road in an unfamiliar place with the daylight going."

Tadek seethed.

"I would like to lodge a formal complaint, your Highness," Tadek said, storming in the door when Evemer *finally* allowed them to go back. Well, attempted to storm. The leg injury made it more of an indignant hop. "I'm being misused *most cruelly.*"

"Oh? How's that?" Kadou said, not putting down the book he was reading. He was lounging on one of the divans in one of the last rays of sunshine, and he looked like a piece of art.

"That man—" One of the other kahyalar, Sanem was in the room, so Tadek couldn't say *your husband,* "—wouldn't let me come back to the house."

"I said you could leave whenever you wanted," Evemer said, coming in behind Tadek. "You chose to stay."

"He *manipulated* me. He was *lying* about made-up errands."

"At my request," Kadou said with a sweet smile, setting the book face-down on his chest. "Thank you, Sanem, you can be done for the day."

Sanem nodded, gathering up the mending she had been working on. "Any requests for dinner that I can pass to whoever's on cooking duty, your Highness?"

"Oh, su böreği, if we've got the things for it."

Sanem saluted and went out. As soon as she shut the door behind herself, Evemer immediately knelt beside the divan as Kadou leaned up to meet him in a deep, slow kiss.

Tadek cleared his throat loudly. "Why did you order him to keep me out of the house?"

Kadou broke the kiss, smiling as Evemer perched on the edge of the divan and took his hand. "Well, clearly I didn't want you underfoot."

Suspicious—Kadou had wanted him not-underfoot to the point that he'd interrupt his own honeymoon for the whole afternoon in order to send Tadek off with *Evemer*, who could not be coaxed to change his mind. A cold throb of uncertainty went through him. "Does this have anything to do with that painter who came this morning?"

"Maybe. There might be a present for you after dinner, if you're good."

A present for him. A painter. And that *confession* he'd made to Kadou the other night.

He didn't want to hope. He didn't want to even think the *word* hope; he certainly didn't want to... anticipate, guess, *long* for what it might be.

(A copy of her portrait? But the painter had only been here a day, and it was a large painting, so probably not a full-size copy, since that could take days or weeks... A smaller one in watercolors, maybe? Small enough to keep in his things, or hang in his room in

Kadou's residence at the palace? As long as it was good enough to see that it was *her*. . .)

"Alright." He swallowed hard. "I was good today. Ask Evemer."

"He was," Evemer said immediately. "He was very mindful of his duty as armsman."

On any other day, Tadek would have scoffed it off and forced Evemer to throw him under the carriage, as the saying went. Irritating to let somebody else be the bigger man. "There. There, you see." Kadou smiled at him—his mother's smile, sparkling eyes and laughing mouth and all, and Tadek couldn't help but add, "I can be more good. We've got an hour or so until dinner. I can guard the door for you if you'd like some. . . privacy."

"My," Kadou marveled. "Attentive to his duties *and* tactful, rather than suggestive or outright lewd."

Evemer stood abruptly. "Guarding the door would be appreciated, thank you, armsman."

"You got it," Tadek chirped and, edging towards slightly manic, hopped himself urgently out of the room.

He wasn't going to hope. He wasn't going to envision it. He wasn't going to think about where he was going to put it. It might not be a painting at all. Maybe the painter had been summoned for some other project that Kadou wanted done, like a life size nude study of Evemer—not that Kadou needed a portrait of that when he could have the real thing nearly whenever he wanted.

He thought about literally anything else. Tasks to do for the rest of the day—tidying their Highnesses' chambers, and refilling their supply of oil, and surreptitiously laundering the bedsheets himself rather than sending them out just in case they had any incriminating evidence on them—and while he was at it, he ought to drag their Highnesses' bedframe six inches or so away from the wall, or at least stuff a pillow behind it to muffle the, ah, impacts—goodness, Evemer seemed to be putting his back into it, good for him—

Kadou, with the kind of mercilessly sadistic *sincerity* that made Tadek want to roll up into a ball like a bug, had dinner served up in the little study rather than at the dining table downstairs. Not only that, but he'd apparently decided it would be a private dinner, just him and Evemer and Tadek.

They ate a low table by the fireplace with the portrait of her hanging over them. Kadou—maybe not merciless after all, maybe in possession of just one singular scrap of mercy—did not give any other indication that it was a special dinner. He didn't make any speeches, he didn't ask Tadek to make any, he didn't offer any toasts. . . They just ate, and Kadou flirted with his husband until Tadek had gotten his bearings and determined that no one was going to try to make a *fuss* of this. It was just dinner, and his Highness could have dinner wherever he wished.

There were no boxes or cloth-wrapped packages, nothing that could have been a painting. Tadek pulled himself together with a vengeance and tried to be pleasant company. He had the training for it, after all—all those lessons in comportment and elocution and polite conversation.

They finished eating, and Kadou sat back with a satisfied sigh—he'd polished off a respectable portion of the su böreği. He was looking so much healthier these days, with color in his cheeks and less of that drawn, solemn look he'd had so often for. . . well, as long as Tadek had ever known him, really. His eyes were brighter, his hair somehow even shinier (not that it needed to be any shinier). Amazing what effect could be had by a few weeks of getting consistently, magnificently laid and some proper meals, instead of glumly picking at his food like a bird.

Kadou turned to him. "Armsman."

Tadek swallowed the lump in his throat. "Yes, your Highness."

"I have a gift for you. You should have had it years ago, and I'm sorry that it has come this late."

Kadou took something from his pocket, something small, wrapped in one of his handkerchiefs. Tadek had kept *her* handkerchief until it fell apart, and then he'd kept the rags of it until it was unrecognizable—he shouldn't have taken it out to rub it between his fingers so much, he shouldn't have wept onto it so often. . .

The thing Kadou was sliding across the table to him was too small to be a painting. Which meant Tadek was entirely unprepared, entirely unguarded for whatever this was. He was terrified.

He picked it up—heavy. Heavy, weighty, made of metal, because he could hear the clink of something shifting inside. He unfolded the handkerchief and found. . .

An oval-shaped pendant made of silver, engraved with fancy floral motifs. It was about the length of his index finger, and it had a substantial woven-ring chain to hang it from, and it was oddly thick for just a pendant—

He turned it over in his hand and saw the hinge on one edge, the latch on the other. A locket. His heart stuttered in his chest and he swallowed carefully, not looking at either of them, willing himself to keep his composure as he opened it with trembling hands.

"Be careful," Kadou murmured. "I'm given to understand the paint will take a while to dry."

It was a painting after all. A miniature copy of that portrait on the wall, done in oil alla prima. It wasn't as refined or detailed as the full-scale portrait, of course, but the colors and shapes had been replicated exactly, and the painter had somehow managed to capture her expression beautifully, even though it was done in such incredibly *minute* detail.

It wasn't quite exact. The painter had only had one day to work on it, after all. The portrait above them was regal and reserved, even with that sparkle to her eyes. The one in the locket looked the littlest bit merrier, as if she were about to burst out laughing at any moment. It was her. It was *her*.

And not on a canvas that he would have had to hang in his room and only see during the brief moments he was there to change clothes or before he blew the candle out and went to sleep. Not on paper, which he would have had to keep tucked in a book to protect it, or buried in his belongings, or paid to have framed.

A locket, one that he could wear and carry around with him wherever he went. And the chain was long enough that she would be hanging over his heart, right in the center of his chest.

Kadou reached out and silently took his hand, squeezing tight. Tadek squeezed back.

The two of them. Fuck, the two of them, her and her son. How could two people be so kind? Twice now, twice in his life he had been living in misery and loneliness so familiar that he could no longer even perceive that it was there, and each time, one of them had seen and offered, with open hands, kindness in silver. The two of them—devastatingly kind, devastatingly perceptive, generous beyond measure, and each in possession of a big enough heart that there was space even for Tadek—raggedy, dust-stained old Tadek—to curl up in a corner by the hearth and be warm.

He sniffled, because the alternative was to drip snot all over himself and the table and the locket. Kadou squeezed his hand again.

He ought to say something. He knew what he wanted to say, but.
. .

He looked down at the picture and thought about the promises he'd made to her, and the ones he'd had to give up, the ones he'd kept for twenty fucking years in silence.

She'd forgive him, for giving up this one now—for releasing his grip and letting it go, remembering it but not holding onto it so tightly. She'd forgive him—she would have even granted him her blessing, if he could have asked her to release him from this oath, and she would have been happy and proud to do so. He knew she would have. After all, she'd wanted him to be a playmate for her little Kadouçiğim, and an armsman was almost the same thing.

She was smiling at him from that locket. *Do your best,* she'd said, and by the gods, he'd tried. Every step of the way, he'd tried. *Always, my lady,* he thought back to her.

He knew what to say—the only thing that could be said, with the weight of this silver in his hands.

"Thank you," he said, his voice cracking. "Thank you, my lord."

Also By Alexandra Rowland

OTHER WORKS:

In The End

Finding Faeries

"In Our Own Image: Radical Empathy, Trickster Gods, and the
Importance of Being Irritating"

The Writer's Oracle Deck

About the Author

Alexandra Rowland is the author of more than a dozen works, including *A Taste of Gold and Iron*, *A Conspiracy of Truths*, and *Running Close to the Wind* (forthcoming June 2024 from Tor.Com Publishing), an educator, and a Hugo Award-nominated podcaster, all sternly supervised by their feline quality control manager. They hold a degree in world literature, mythology, and folklore from Truman State University.

Find them and more of their work at their website, www.alexandrarowland.net, where you can sign up for their newsletter to be notified about new releases or join their official Discord server to meet other fans. You can also find them at:

Instagram and other Socials: @_alexrowland

Patreon: www.patreon.com/_alexrowland

Ko-fi: www.ko-fi.com/ariaste